Imee
Mother of the Messiah

Deanna Malespin

Copyright © 2019 Deanna Malespin

All rights reserved.

ISBN: 978-965-92800-1-8

DEDICATION

I dedicate this book to the amazing women who have made their decision to follow God's call on their lives, even when it means great sacrifice.

CONTENTS

I Am Miriam

	Acknowledgments	i
	Author's Notes	ii
1	Hidden	1
2	Exposed	19
3	Boldness	35
4	A Home	49
5	The Lamb	58
6	Make Way	71
7	The Ring & the Doxology	85
8	Unexpected	97
9	The Past	109
10	Immanuel	121
	Scripture References	144

ACKNOWLEDGMENTS

This is the first book I have written and I could not have done this on my own. First, I wish to thank my husband Chaim, my favourite guy in the world! He has always encouraged me to follow my dreams and is a source of loving support for me. I am so blessed to have him in my life!

I wish to thank my family who have all been so encouraging! My parents read it and gave me a 'thumbs up'! Their enthusiasm helped fuel me all through this journey.

I also wish to thank my dear friends who have been so encouraging and supportive along the way. Writing a book for the first time has been like navigating through the dark, and their prayers and positive words have given me strength. And Sarah Gasiorowski, thank you for reading one of the first drafts! Your feedback really helped me along the way!

Julie Gray, thank you for your professional feedback; your input helped me make a decision on which direction I should go with the book. https://www.juliegray.info

To Fiverr (https://www.fiverr.com) - Thanks to the two editors who helped edit my grammar and polish the story. I am so grateful. Highly recommend Kevin: https://www.fiverr.com/kevin100percent

And most importantly, I thank God for the inspiration for the book! More thoughts on this in my Author's Note

AUTHOR'S NOTES

So glad to connect with you here. I just want to say a few words before you dive into this story.

Some things you should know: this book is fictional, but it is based on the story of Miriam (Mary) and Joseph. The Bible provides us with the baby announcement and a snippet about her visit with Elizabeth, but then there is this big gap between then and when the baby is born. My story helps fill in the blanks! But note, I am not a historian nor theologian. So if you are looking for factual/actual information here, this is not the best source! A lot of inspired imagination was used in the joyful writing of this story. I must tell you, sometimes it was hard to come up with some of the conclusions I had to decide upon. For example, the timing of Yeshua's (Jesus') birth. When I inquired of Google, there was a heap of information to the point of being overwhelmed! So I researched sources as best I could, and chose a season and time, But in the end, I don't know 100% if it is the actual birthdate of Yeshua.

The inspiration for this story came to me when I watched a cartoon video of the story of Miriam with my children. Like you, I have seen numerous movies, cartoons, listened to audiotapes and read the Christmas story many times. But in this particular cartoon version, Miriam was holding a broom! I don't know why, but this changed the whole story for me! Seeing her with a broom suddenly made her like a regular woman, like me and all of my female readers. I guess I had always felt a distance from Miriam, an arm's length relationship from the Holy mother of our Lord. But my image of her as an untouchable porcelain statue shattered when I saw her with a broom, and all of a sudden, I could relate to her. From there, the whole story came alive for me, and now

I am so passionate about this story, I pray everyone will read it! And trust me, it is a dramatic story!

Something I really wanted to incorporate in the narrative is a sense of context, bringing you in to the times, traditions, culture and customs that abounded where and when Miriam lived. She was a young Jewish woman living under the tight rule of the Roman Empire. This brought in a myriad of things Miriam had to deal with as a wife and mother under foreign rule. This aspect of her life is often lacking in the traditional Christmas story. So I have woven it into mine. And since I live and am raising my family in Israel, the place where this story takes place, I have brought in the geography as the land here in Israel also tells the story. For example, I had to research how long it would take for her to travel from Nazareth to Judea where her cousin Elizabeth lived. This was a fascinating journey that left me admiring Miriam for her stamina!

You will notice in the story that I am not following the idea that Miriam was a 14-16 year-old young maiden. I found that season of my life so awkward and confusing, I simply cannot relate to being that age and being in the season of marriage and babies! So I took the liberty of setting her age at about 18 years old. The Bible doesn't say how old she was, so it is simply a guess on my part.

Also, since living in Israel, I've learned that the name Yeshua is Jesus' Hebrew name. It means 'salvation.' And Mary's Hebrew name is Miriam. I suppose because I am living here in Israel, these names roll off my tongue more easily. However, I didn't want to change all of the names so as to not make the story completely foreign from the traditional one. So I hope it doesn't seem strange for you.

As for Joseph, in the book you will discover a 'back-story' about him that I have imagined up and it may be surprising to you. It's also not factual, but perhaps a possibility? I'll let you be the judge.

The profits from this book will be going to some of the local charities that I personally know here in the land. So by purchasing this book, you will be blessing some Israeli organisations and the people they minister to.

I hope you will enjoy this unique version of the Christmas story! Be blessed!

Deanna Malespin
chaim.deanna@gmail.com

1 HIDDEN

Miriam pulled her beige wool dress in close around her abdomen and slowly ran her hand down over the contour of her small expanding belly. Only she could really tell that her belly had grown a little. She sighed as she looked down at her stomach. How could this be? she wondered to herself. How could this even be possible? She stood sideways in front of a blurry, rectangular mirror that hung in her parents' bedroom. Her small frame showed a slender glimpse of an emerging bump.

Miriam's mind wandered back a couple of months ago, to the pivotal moment her whole life seemed to have been turned upside down.

2 months earlier

It had been a busy week with hectic preparations for her upcoming wedding. Weddings in her small village were always a big deal. Her dear beloved Joseph would come for her as the sun would begin to set behind the rolling hills around her small village of Nazareth, and there would be a whole special procession with Joseph leading the way. He would come to her parents' home to come for his bride! She and her family would follow Joseph to their new home. Then there would be the ceremony, followed by a huge feast with non-stop music and dancing!

She couldn't wait! Anticipation and excitement filled her heart and mind. She often found herself daydreaming about the wedding and life with her soon-to-be husband!

But for now the mundane chores and cares of life took over. Miriam was at her family home alone working through her chores. For the moment, the house was empty, and it was just Miriam at home. The fire roared happily in the fireplace bringing warmth into the home during the cold rainy winter season. She had just finished preparing the evening meal for her family while her mother and sister were off at the market picking up a few more items to complete the meal. Her father and brothers were in the olive press checking on the pickled olives. The olive harvest had finished about a month ago, and since then it had been a very busy season of pressing the olives and then preparing the olive oil for the market.

She began sweeping the floor of the main part of the house that included the kitchen and the sitting area with a low wooden table where Miriam and her family would gather for their meals, and where they would extend hospitality to their guests. She hummed to herself happily. It had just been a few months ago that Miriam had been betrothed to her beloved Joseph. She was in love! And she was very lucky to be in love too. Usually, marriage arrangements were decided upon by the parents of both the bride-to-be and groom-to-be. Other times it was between a father of a young lady and a suitor. If a young lady found favor in a potential suitor, he would go directly to the father where they would discuss the dowry, and between the two of them, come to some kind of agreement for the marriage. There were cases where the young lady wasn't even interested in her betrothed and had to learn to love her husband through the course of their marriage. But for Miriam, as soon as she had laid eyes on Joseph, she felt her heart flutter like a million butterflies, and to her delight she had also caught the eye of the handsome young carpenter from Bethlehem. He had moved up north to Nazareth to work with his uncle in his shop. He was making good progress in the shop, and the business excelled with Joseph's partnership. He was a very hard worker, and his attention to detail brought him a lot of business. Miriam enjoyed his company very much. He was intelligent and a deep thinker, but was also adventurous and hilarious. He treated her with respect and kindness, and was just fun to be around. He wasn't like some of the simple-minded farmers in the area or the stuffy, business-minded people she had known growing up in Nazareth. He was cultured and down-to-earth, and altogether a very good man. Perhaps his only fault was being a bit of a perfectionist and overly responsible and cautious, which often comes naturally for the eldest child in a family.

As she swept the floor, she began imagining herself cleaning her own home. Joseph was still in the process of building their new home where they would begin their lives together. She couldn't wait for it to be done. Once the house was complete, it meant that their impending wedding would commence any day.

Her thoughts were then suddenly interrupted by a knock on the door. Surprised, Miriam looked up and leaned the broom up against the wall, and opened the heavy wooden door of the house. It creaked and groaned as she opened it wide. To her surprise, a man in a pure white robe, whom she had never met before, stood there. He was tall and handsome with a friendly face and warm eyes.

"Hello, please come in." Miriam ushered him in with a bow of her head. White clothing was a sign of wealth, so she assumed that he was perhaps a businessman. "My father will be home soon. I can make you a cup of tea as you wait for him." Miriam welcomed the stranger into the family home. He followed her inside, and she gestured for him to sit down on the pillows next to the low table. With her father's olive oil business, merchants often came by the house to purchase olive oil to sell in markets all over Judea and Samaria, and sometimes even in the Decapolis.

He looked over in the direction of where she gestured for him to rest, but instead of moving in that direction he turned back and looked at Miriam directly in the eye. "Rejoice, highly-favored one!" the man said with excitement.

Miriam was taken aback.

But before she could decipher what the man even meant, he continued to speak. "The Lord is with you; blessed are you among women!"

Miriam raised her eyebrows and looked at the man even more quizzically. *This greeting seemed very unusual,* Miriam thought.

Then the man laid his hands on her shoulders and looked at her and smiled again.

She felt awkward at first, but somehow she felt as if she could trust him, and didn't feel threatened by him in any way.

His eyes were bright and shining. "Do not be afraid, Miriam, for you have found favor with God."

Now Miriam was even more taken aback. *How did he know her name?* Then stories from the Torah that she had heard the Rabbis read aloud in her synagogue came to mind. The story where God met with Abraham in his tent, or when an angel met with Joshua and gave him instructions to march around Jericho seven times. *Could this be an angel?* she wondered. She wrestled with the thought. *Surely not! That would be crazy!* But somehow this man in white fit the description of an angel. *Could it be possible that God had a message for her?*

The man continued. "Behold, you will conceive in your womb and bring forth a Son and shall call His name Yeshua. He will be great, and will be called the Son of the Highest, and the Lord God will give Him the throne of His father, David. And he will reign over the house of Jacob forever, and of His kingdom there shall be no end."

Miriam's eyes grew wide and her arms burned with goosebumps. "How can this be?" she asked, taking a step back, trying to process this incredible message from the man whom she now really thought was an angel. She placed her hand on her belly. *She was going to have a baby? Conceive? But not just any baby... the Messiah! The promised Messiah who was prophesied about by the prophets and whom her people longed for! The one who would restore the Kingdom of Israel!*

At that time, the Roman Empire extended far and wide, including the land of Israel. Her people longed for the Messiah to come and save them! Every Friday evening before shabbat, the community would gather in the local synagogue for prayers and scripture readings, and each time they were reminded about the promised seed of salvation. This seed, which was first spoken about in the Garden of Eden, which was then passed down through the fathers, Abraham, Isaac, and Jacob, and then continued to be spoken about by the prophets, was to be the Messiah. Her people longed for Him. And what a better time to come than now when her people were burdened by the tyranny of the Roman Empire.

Then Miriam's mind turned toward the practical aspects. *How was it going to work, since she was not yet married?* And even though she was to be married, she would not sleep with Joseph until their wedding night. Would the promise be able to wait until they would be properly married? "How can this be, since I do not know any man?" Miriam asked the angel with curiosity.

"The Holy Spirit will come upon you, and the power of the Most High will overshadow you; also, that Holy One who is to be born shall be called the Son of God," the angel explained.

Miriam nodded slowly, not really understanding what he meant exactly. *Overshadow her? The Son of God will come through her womb?*

"Now indeed, Elizabeth your relative has also conceived a son in her old age; and this is now the sixth month for her who was called barren. For with God, nothing is impossible," the angel added a note of encouragement.

Miriam listened in wonder to the angel's words. She remembered the stories of the mighty women of God whom she had heard about from the Torah. Her favorite story was about Queen Esther who had been called by God for a special mission, and fearlessly made an appeal for her people, even in the face of possible death. Who was she to say no to the bidding of God?

Miriam looked into the angel's joyful eyes. "Behold the maidservant of the Lord! Let it be to me according to your word," she said with boldness and confidence.

The man took Miriam's hand and kissed it. "God bless you." Then with that, he departed out the door.

As the door shut behind him, Miriam nearly fell back onto one of the stools. What had just happened? Her heart beat wildly inside of her. She had just encountered an angel of God who came specifically to give her a message from on High! Her mind raced as she tried to process the incredible message given to her by the angel. She was going to be the mother of the Messiah!? Excitement welled up inside her heart! The Messiah was coming!

However, little did she know the impact this visitation would have on her life.

That same evening, after the visitation, she was eager to announce the good news to her family. Miriam waited for when they would all be together, seated around the dinner table. She could hardly contain the news within her! She could just imagine how thrilled they would be! All of her life, growing up in a very traditional family, learning the stories of the Torah, they often spoke of the Messiah to come who would bring salvation to her people and reign once again on David's throne as the prophets had foretold. Miriam knew they would be ecstatic to hear that the Messiah was indeed coming and that she had been chosen and highly favored by God to carry the Son of God in her womb.

As the sun was going down, casting warm, reddish hues of light through the window of their home, the family gathered around the table. Her mother Anna was dishing out cooked barley and lentils with crushed nuts on top into clay bowls. Her father sat at the head of the table discussing the family business with the two older sons, Samuel and Simon. Hannah, Miriam's younger sister, poured water into clay cups for each person. Once all the food was dished out, her father picked up the loaf of bread and lifted it in the air and mumbled a quick blessing over the food. Then everyone began to partake of the meal. Miriam looked around at her family with a big smile on her face. She couldn't hold in the news any longer and stood up in front of everyone.

Everyone looked up at her in surprise.

"Dearest Miriam, do you have somewhere to go?" her father Heli looked up at his daughter with a questioning look on his face.

She beamed with excitement. "I have the best news in the whole wide world, Abba!" she exclaimed.

"And what is that, my dear?" her father asked with a smile in return.

"The Messiah is coming!" Miriam declared.

No one responded at first. They seemed a bit stunned at the news. Her brothers, Simon and Samuel broke the silence by chuckling softly at her abruptness.

Miriam ignored them, and continued, "I am going to be the mother of the Messiah!"

"The mother of the Messiah? *You?*" Samuel her brother asked.

"Yes. You see, earlier today while everyone was out, a man all dressed in white came here to tell me the news. He was an angel. I saw an angel! He told me that I am going to conceive the Son of God and I am to call Him Yeshua!" Miriam said enthusiastically.

She looked around the table at her parents and siblings with a big smile on her face. But as she did, she was surprised that their response to the good news didn't seem to match her height of excitement. She thought that they would be jumping up and down in joy to rejoice with her! But instead, they stared at her, dumbfounded.

"An angel came to our house and told you that you were going to be the mother of the Messiah?" Samuel tried to comprehend Miriam's message.

"How can you be a mother if you are not even married yet?" Simon piped in.

"I will be married very soon." Miriam frowned at his question.

"Darling… why don't you first get married, then you can talk about having babies," her mother chided. "First things first."

"Mother!" Miriam retorted. "An angel visited me today! This is a big deal!"

"Who told you this again?" her sister Hannah asked.

"This man in white told me. An angel came to our house today!" Miriam repeated herself again. She looked at her father in hopes that he would, at least, share her excitement. Miriam knew no one else that prayed and longed for the Messiah more than her father. Surely, he believed her.

"Please, my dear, sit down. Sounds like a very wonderful message, but let's leave it to God to bring the Messiah," Heli, her father, commanded gently.

"But Abba, he said that *I* would give birth to the Messiah! The Son of David," Miriam pressed further.

"Miriam, sit down and do not talk about this anymore," her father commanded again, this time a little more firmly. "If you start talking like this around the town, people will think you are crazy. If it is from God, then it will happen. If not, then pursue peace by not uttering such declarations."

Miriam humbly sat down, very disappointed by her family's response. It was not what she had expected at all. For the first time in her life, she felt alone. She ate her food quietly, fighting back the tears that threatened to fall.

The next day, Miriam decided she would try to tell Joseph. Surely, he would believe her and be excited, especially at the prospect of being the father of the Messiah!

Joseph was in his shop sanding down a dining room table when she walked in. He looked up at her with his gorgeous brown eyes. He was tall with an olive complexion and was very handsome. He wore a tan-colored robe with a scarlet sash tied around his waist that Miriam had made for him. He had a trimmed dark beard and a curly mop of dark hair. The short sleeves of his robe revealed his strong buff arms. He swept his dark curly hair off his forehead and smiled at her.

"My beautiful Miriam!" He wiped the sawdust from his calloused hands with a rag that hung from a peg. Then he quickly circled the table to Miriam and lifted her up in the air and twirled her around. For a moment, she almost forgot why she had come to his shop.

"Believe it or not, I am working on *our* table! But that is my secret. What's your secret?" he said, playfully tapping her on the nose. Then he ran his fingers through her long dark hair and looked at her lovingly.

"I do have something to tell you," Miriam said as she remembered her mission to tell him the good news.

"Of course you do!" Joseph released her as he leaned back against the wall and smiled. "I am always here for you, my dear, and I would love to hear whatever you have to tell me."

"Well…I just received a message from God." Miriam paused to watch his reaction. The playful look in his eyes turned serious. She took a deep breath and then spoke, "We are going to have the Messiah." Miriam looked at him closely trying to read every sign of body language before he could even respond with his words. Joseph cocked his head to one side and raised his eyebrows in wonder.

"That's quite a message. From God, you say?" Joseph asked intently. Joseph took Miriam's hand in his.

"Yes, a man in white clothing came to my father's house and told me that I would conceive and have a Son and will name him Yeshua," Miriam said.

"I would like to meet this man. How dare he put ideas in your head without talking to me first!" Joseph looked annoyed.

"Joseph, you believe me, right?" Miriam asked hopefully, ignoring his complaint.

"Believe what? That we are going to have a baby? For sure, I hope we have lots of babies!" Joseph smiled. "If one of them becomes the Messiah, then that would be great. But first, I just want to marry you. So why are we talking about children right now? For now, let's just focus on preparing for our wedding." He pushed the subject aside. Miriam started to protest, but Joseph pressed his finger against her lips to shush her. "The next time any man comes by telling you hypothetical things, then send them to me," he said, seriously. "I mean it. It is very dangerous to say what you just said! There are people willing to kill one another over the subject of the Messiah! And if the Romans caught word of this madness, then your life could be in danger!"

Miriam sighed. If only the angel had come to the house when her family and Joseph had been home. Now the whole event with the angel felt like it was just a dream. Only time would tell if she would have the Messiah or not.

She decided after that moment, that there was no point in telling people the good news, as no one seemed to believe her. They would just have to find out when it happened.

In her mind, she had assumed that upon her wedding night, she would conceive the Messiah with Joseph. It made sense, and it would make sense to everyone else around her. She carried on with her usual business, looking even more forward to her marriage union with the man she loved.

Back to the present day

Now about two months later since the visitation from the angel, she found herself in the most unusual situation. Miriam swept her long thick wavy brown hair over her shoulder. She looked at herself again in the mirror. Her large beautiful brown eyes, under a canopy of thick black eyelashes, looked anxiously back at her. What was she going to do? She was now in a very precarious position which only she knew about.

A couple of weeks after the visitation, when she would usually go to the mikvah with her sister Hannah to cleanse herself after her week of impurity, her flow had not shown up, to her surprise. As was prescribed in the Torah for every Jewish woman, after one's monthly cycle was complete, the women would go to the mikvah to become ceremonially clean again. At first, Miriam thought that maybe her period was just late. Then as time went on and her flow still had not come, the thought struck her suddenly that perhaps she could somehow already be pregnant? Maybe when the angel said that the Holy Spirit would overshadow her, he meant that she would just conceive supernaturally. She wrestled with the idea and tried to find other reasons why she might have missed her cycle. The thought of conceiving before marriage scared her. However, she didn't want to jump to conclusions. Her mother had told her that it was normal to skip a period during stressful or busy times; and maybe with the wedding preparations, it caused her to skip her period. Miriam prayed that it was so.

Then the next month when her sister's flow began again, Miriam was again surprised that hers still had not yet come. She had always been in sync with her sister, with maybe only a day or two apart at most. And now on top of that, she started to feel other things like nausea and fatigue, and her appetite seemed to have changed … She knew from her friends who were already married and having children that these were common symptoms of pregnancy.

Being pregnant while only betrothed was deeply frowned upon by her people. The customs and the standard that they struggled to live by according to the Torah would relegate her in society to a life of shame if her secret were to ever be exposed. It could even mean being stoned to death if they would judge her as adulterous. She was scared to tell Joseph, her beloved betrothed. Would he still take her as his wife? She had felt like she was the luckiest girl in the world to be betrothed to the most eligible handsome young man in the town. But now what? This little secret could unravel her magical love story, which she was very much afraid of.

Not wanting to bring attention to herself, she pretended that her period had also come and went to the mikvah with her sister and went through the motions as if she was going through the cleansing. She needed time to think about what to do and figure out how everything should play out.

It was difficult to hide her secret from her family. Growing up, Miriam had always been carefree, strong, and confident. She was known for being outgoing, bold and a little bit sassy, but never overboard, because on the other hand, she was very kind, tender-hearted, caring for others and thoughtful. She felt terrible about hiding something from her family when all her life they had always been very close to one another and very honest to each other. Never before had she ever hid anything from them. She tried her best to carry on with normal life and wedding preparations as if nothing was ailing her. Thankfully, because of the wedding preparations, her family seemed to assume that she was just tired because of the upcoming wedding. Or at least Miriam hoped that was the case.

Just the other month, one of the young girls in town had become pregnant after being raped by one of the Roman soldiers that patrolled the region around her town. Miriam's heart broke for her. Coming from a very traditional Jewish town, this meant a lifetime of shame. She would probably never be married, and her baby would be considered a bastard since it came from a non-Jewish father. The whole town was still gossiping about the scenario. If anyone would find out she too was pregnant outside of marriage, it could mean the end of everything she had ever hoped for. Joseph would most likely divorce her, and she would be put in the same situation or worse. She could even be stoned to death, depending on the decision of the Pharisees in the town. She was unable to come up with an idea on how to convince others that she had become pregnant by divine means. If her family and Joseph wouldn't even believe the angel's announcement, how would they believe her that she was already pregnant with the Messiah?

"Miriam?" Joseph's voice came echoing from outside her family home, interrupting her thoughts.

Quickly Miriam loosened her grip on her dress. In as calm a voice as she could muster, to hide the anxiety in her heart, she called back to him, "I'll be right there, my love." She sighed deeply. Somehow she had to let him know the truth of her situation.

2 EXPOSED

"Miriam, my dear, come for a walk with me." Miriam's father opened up his arm to her.

They were outside their two-story stone and clay family home, where Miriam was just finishing her chores with the animals. The stable and the house was connected with a corridor in between the two sections and a courtyard in the middle for the chickens and the lambs to roam free. She had just freshened up the lamb stalls and the cow stall with fresh, sweet-smelling hay and had filled the water troughs full of water and the feeding troughs with grains and hay. She looked up nervously at her father. Whenever he had something important to talk to her about, he would invite her for a walk. Her heart began to beat wildly inside of her. Somehow, at that moment, she knew that *he* knew that she was pregnant. The dreaded moment had come. She swallowed slowly, trying to slow down her breathing. "Yes Abba," she said as her voice trembled a little. She stood up and entered under his welcoming arm.

They walked together to the olive grove behind the house. It was a beautiful sunny spring day, with birds singing as they flew from tree to tree. Miriam envied them for their carefree lives. Her father made small talk all along the way. He recounted the story of how his grandfather had bought the olive grove a long time ago. She knew the story almost by heart but loved to hear it nonetheless. But this time, Miriam's mind raced with anxiety which inhibited her from hearing the familiar words. Part of her dreaded any questions her father might ask, but the other half of her begged for the truth to be revealed so she could be free again – like the birds she had just seen.

They walked towards the bench – one her father had made – under one of the olive trees that overlooked the rolling hills, offering a gorgeous display of nature in front of them. Miriam gazed into the distance. The words of one of the psalms came to her mind, "I look to the hills, where does my help come from? My help comes from the Lord, maker of heaven and earth!" The beauty of nature and the verse of the psalm helped to calm her nerves a little. Her father gestured for them to sit down. Miriam sank onto the bench next to her father.

Silence.

She glanced over at her father. She knew he must be thinking how to approach the subject. He stroked his long thick grey beard thoughtfully as he looked towards the beautiful hills. "Do you remember the 'angel' you told us about?" he finally asked, breaking the silence.

Miriam slowly nodded. She had wondered if her father had even remembered the night she had made her big declaration that the Messiah was coming and that she was to be the mother, because no one had ever spoken about it again.

But now, clearly, he had remembered. He cleared his throat. "Your mother seems to think that your behavior is a bit peculiar, almost as if you might be …" Miriam's eyes widened and looked up at her father; she could feel her eyes burn as they filled with tears. They had noticed!

Her father continued. "Did this person in white clothing who came to visit you, did he … touch you?" he asked, slowly and gently.

Miriam stood up in shock. She was not prepared for a question like this! He had it all wrong! But how could she explain and convince someone of something that has never happened to any other woman? "Abba, he did not touch me like you are thinking! I don't know what to say! You and Mother and the whole family didn't believe me when I told you that the angel gave me a divine message –"

"Miriam, have you and Joseph … fornicated?" he continued to investigate.

"No!" Miriam exclaimed. "Abba, I have never known a man, but as the angel said, I would conceive the Son of the Living God," she blurted.

She felt like the raging waters within her heart had suddenly burst through the gates.

"That's impossible," her father scowled.

"With God nothing is impossible," Miriam repeated the words of the angel. "Abba, you must believe me, the Messiah is inside of me!"

"So you say you are pregnant … so who did you sleep with?" her father probed further.

"Abba, the angel told me that the Holy Spirit would overshadow me!" Miriam almost shouted.

"What nonsense! I know how children are made; your mother and I made four babies! For God's sake, Miriam, speak the truth!" her father shouted back angrily.

"I *am* telling only the truth!" she exclaimed exasperatedly.

"Do you know what it means to sleep with someone before marriage?" Her father stood up in a fury. "Do you know the shame that this brings to my household?"

"You have no idea the anguish I have in my soul!" Miriam began to cry. "I did not know that it would be like this …"

"Does Joseph know that you are pregnant?" her father asked.

"No… I also tried to tell him about the message from the angel but he said the same thing, he said that we should talk about children *after* marriage," Miriam replied as she wiped away falling tears with the edge of her sleeve.

"You are days away from your wedding, and you are pregnant!" her father exclaimed as if trying to convince himself of the ridiculous news. He rubbed his face with his hands and pulled on his beard nervously. "And you wouldn't tell us outright!?"

"How could I? What if Joseph abandons me?"

"And what? Is Joseph going to marry a pregnant bride? You want to surprise him? Miriam, you are not thinking!" He shook his finger in her face. "You can't expect me to believe this blasphemy that you are pregnant without a man. Did the *air* make you pregnant? You foolish girl! Let's go back inside, and I do not want you to leave the house until I have figured out what to do with you!" He grabbed Miriam's arm and walked her back to the house hurriedly. Miriam cried the whole way home.

Once they got to the house, she ran up the stairs to her room and fell on her bed and continued to sob. She could hear her father yelling anxiously and her mother's voice responding back with even more anxiety and concern.

The truth was out. At least, the part that she was pregnant. The part about her being pregnant without knowing a man and carrying the Messiah was not received as Miriam assumed it would be.

Miriam held her hand to heart; she felt like it had been torn in two. She loved her family dearly, and it pained her to be the cause of any fury and shame. "God, why didn't this happen after my wedding?" she cried through her tears. "Did you mean to ruin my life?"

All her life, she felt a love for God in her heart and desired to respect and walk according to the Torah and follow its commands. Growing up in the small village of Nazareth, only the boys went to school in the local synagogue where the Rabbis would teach them how to read and write. They would teach them mathematics, science, history, and lessons from the Torah. Miriam had been caught several times as she was growing up, sitting below the synagogue window listening to the lessons. She had always wished she could also join in the lessons, especially hearing about her people's history and the stories from the Torah. It was interesting for her to hear the stories of how David slew the giant Goliath, or how Daniel survived being thrown into the lions' den. She believed that God was real and that He did perform miracles for her people. She knew that what was happening to her was a miracle from God. She was enthusiastic about the idea of being chosen amongst all women for the divine task of being the mother of the Messiah, but she hadn't expected the sacrifice.

Miriam's heart sank. Her father was probably going to tell Joseph. Her worst fear. It had been very difficult to hide the pregnancy from Joseph. She felt a little withdrawn from him, but he was very busy building their new house, so she hoped he hadn't noticed. She was wishful in hoping that perhaps after their wedding, she could say that she conceived the baby with him, as this would eliminate the ruffling of the town's feathers. But Joseph was taking a long time in building their new house. He wanted it to be perfect. And with each passing day, her wishful thinking seemed to become more and more impossible.

Miriam heard a strange noise. She sat up to listen. It sounded like someone was crying. She stood up and walked to the entrance of her bedroom and peeked down the stairs to the main room. She saw her parents embracing each other while both of them were crying on each other's shoulders. Fresh tears filled Miriam's eyes. She cupped her face in her hands and wept. All her life, she had always tried hard to make her parents proud; bringing shame to her family was the last thing she had ever wanted to do. If anything, she had hoped this divine mission would bring her and her family honor. If only they would believe her! Now more than ever her people were searching and longing for the Messiah. The current political landscape left them under the iron fist of the Roman Empire. At present, King Herod was the king of Judea, but he was really just a puppet in the hands of the Romans. He did allow religious freedom and the ability for people to practice their own traditions, but they were very unhappy with the Roman occupation and longed to be set free! The taxes were burdensome and caused many to lose their land, homes, and dignity. Rome ruled ruthlessly and many were afraid of them.

They also spread their pagan practices and culture that many people abhorred. There was a constant struggle between the Jewish population and their Roman occupiers.

Miriam hoped the Messiah would be like the Maccabee family. A couple of hundred years ago, when her people were held captive under the Seleucid Empire, their occupiers tried to force them to follow pagan practices and even went so far to attempting to annihilate the Torah from being observed. Many people died for simply wanting to worship freely. They even did the worst thing possible … placed false idols in the Holy Temple in Jerusalem. This was the last straw for her people, and the Maccabee family from the tribe of Levi rose up from amongst the Jewish people and fought a difficult but victorious battle against the Greeks. It was a proud moment in her people's history. However, it was only a short interval of about 100 years of independence until the Romans came in, and not only swept over the land of Israel but all of the Middle East and Egypt.

Unlike many of the other nations, her people held a unique spiritual connection to their land. It was not just a piece of land for them, it was their Promised Land. This meaning came from many generations ago, when the forefathers of the Jewish people, Abraham, Isaac and Jacob, received a covenant from their God that this was to be their land forever. From legends, the Torah and words spoken by their prophets further deepened their connection to their land.

The Torah also set them apart from other nations. One of their spiritual leaders of old, named Moses, had a very special connection to God. And through him, God gave them the Torah. The Torah presented a standard and a code of law for them to follow which they tried their best to do. And from that time on, their history went back and forth of her people following after God or wandering after other gods. When they followed God, they prospered, but whenever they worshipped foreign gods, then they would become weak. The worst and darkest period in their history was when the Babylonian Kingdom overtook Israel and destroyed their Holy Temple and took their people into Babylonian exile. Then, after 70 years, they repented, and many returned back to their homeland in 586 BC (BCE) where they were able to rebuild the second Temple. They were given another chance.

Miriam's father often repeated the stories of the history of her people to her and her family. Because of that, Miriam had grown up with a hope that one day the Messiah would come to save her people and their land.

Miriam spent the rest of the day in her room. She could hear her family going about their usual duties. As the evening was fast approaching, she was beckoned downstairs.

"Miriam, please come downstairs and help me with supper," her mother requested. Miriam slowly walked down the creaky wooden stairs. Her mother was stirring a thick stew over the fireplace. The air was tense and stiff, and her mother refused to make eye contact with her.

"Stir the stew as I prepare the bread," her mother said as she handed the spoon to Miriam. She took it and stirred the stew, making sure not to let the bottom burn over the fire. Her mother turned her attention to kneading the bread dough. They prepared the evening meal together in silence.

Miriam tried to think of something that she could say that would break this uncomfortable silence between her and her mother. Questions whirled around in her mind, making it difficult for her to think of anything worth saying. Was she banished to her room forever? Were her parents going to punish her? Did they decide to tell Joseph? What was going to happen to her now? If they believed that she had slept with another man other than Joseph, then by the law of the Torah, she could be condemned to death. It was against the law of the Torah for a girl to sleep with another man, especially if she was betrothed. Betrothal was highly respected in her community, and it was considered adultery to sleep with another man who is not your betrothed. Somehow, she had to convince them that she was supernaturally pregnant, and had not slept with anyone. Otherwise, her life and the life of the Messiah could be in danger.

Miriam looked at her mother; if she could maybe convince her mother, perhaps she could convince her father, she thought.

"Mother," she said, breaking the silence, "you know that I am being honest when I say that I have never slept with a man."

Her mother whirled around to face her. Her face was flushed with anger. Miriam was shocked by her mother's reaction. "How dare you speak such nonsense!"

"Mother, I am still a virgin!" Miriam insisted.

"Every baby has a father! Don't try to tell me that I don't know what I am talking about. I have become pregnant four times, bless the Lord! And never in my life have I ever heard someone speak such blasphemy," her mother raged.

Miriam had never seen her mother so upset. It shocked her, but she was still motivated to try to persuade her. "I know it seems impossible! But the angel said that with God, nothing is impossible," she said as she tried to hold her ground.

"Tell that to the Rabbis and to Joseph," her mother fumed. "You had everything, my girl, a wonderful future ahead of you! You were one of the brightest and most beautiful girls in this town. Why have you thrown it away? And good gracious, why don't you tell me the truth? Who did you sleep with? Or who cast this evil spell on you that has caused your mind to be deranged?" her mother shouted painfully with tears beginning to roll down her weathered cheeks.

"I am telling you the truth!" Miriam insisted. "I have not slept with any man."

Her mother shook her head. "Go back to your room. I cannot bear this, because you know what the consequences of your actions will be! They are going to stone you for engaging in unlawful sexual relations!"

"No, mother, they can't do that," Miriam's voice cracked. "You must believe me! Please, mother!" Miriam felt panicky. Was her family really going to allow her to be stoned? All of her life she had felt safe and secure in her home. Now she felt completely insecure. If she went to her room, it could be a matter of hours before someone might drag her down, bring her before the Rabbis who would demand that she be stoned to death. If her family wouldn't believe her, then who would? Her family knew her best and loved her the most; if they weren't willing to trust her, then who would?

Miriam was doubtful that Joseph would even believe her. He thought he was marrying a virgin, which was true, but would he want to marry a pregnant virgin? Miriam started to move towards the stairs that led to her room; she glanced over her shoulder to the open entrance to the home. In a split second, she decided to dash out of the house. She picked up the skirt of her robe and quickly ran out of the house.

"Come back here!" her mother shouted behind her. Miriam kept running out of the courtyard, out onto the road and passing the other villagers' homes. She ran towards the pastures where the sheep and goats grazed on the hillsides of Nazareth. She could hear shouting behind her, but like a startled deer, she kept running.

"Miriam!" she suddenly heard Joseph shouting from behind her. She could hear his swift footsteps running behind her, and before she could turn around, she felt a strong hand grab her arm and jerk her around. He was breathing hard as he held her arm firmly, and by the look on his face, she knew he had heard the news.

"We need to talk," Joseph demanded. Miriam was also out of breath and too terrified to say anything, let alone breathe! The moment she had dreaded and had rehearsed in her mind a million times was unraveling.

"I need you to be honest with me," he said slowly and firmly. "Are you ... pregnant?" he asked holding her strongly and looking intently at her.

Miriam slowly nodded.

She watched as his face turned from anger to utter heartbreak. He let go of her and took a few steps back.

"Let me explain ..." Miriam broke the tense silence.

"I thought you loved me? That we had something special together?" Joseph's eyes were filled with rarely-seen tears.

"I adore you!" Miriam fell to her knees and grabbed hold of his hand and tried to kiss it, but he jerked his hand away.

"Don't touch me, you whore!" he yelled.

"It's not what you think!" Miriam implored. "You must believe me, Joseph!" She stood up to plead her case. This might be her last chance so she might as well try to give it all she had. "Joseph, please believe me! An angel came to me with a message, telling me that I was to conceive and bear a child, but not just any child - the Messiah! I told you this already. And that we would name him Yeshua! Then he told me that the Holy Spirit would overshadow me. I thought it meant that I would conceive the Messiah together with you, but I guess it meant that I, without ever knowing a man, would conceive! And now I am miraculously pregnant with the Messiah and am still a virgin." Miriam paused.

By the look on his face, she knew that he didn't believe her.

Discouragement suddenly swept over her like a wave over the seashore, wiping away any trace of hope within her. "I … I love you, Joseph, and want to be your wife. I understand if you don't believe me, because I can hardly believe it myself." Miriam shrugged her shoulders. She could barely look at him now.

He looked so heartbroken as if she had betrayed him.

"I am sorry that I didn't tell you, I didn't want this to happen."

"You are talking complete nonsense, Miriam!" Joseph shouted at her. "All of this Messiah talk has caused you to go mad! Fess up to the truth, Miriam; you are either lying to me about not sleeping with this 'messenger' who somehow brainwashed you. Or you were raped by one of the Roman centurions, and you refuse to confess the truth!"

"I know this doesn't make sense, and I do sound mad … but I have always and will always tell you the truth." Miriam said firmly. "But I beg you for mercy, dear Joseph, that you spare me and the Messiah from being stoned," she implored.

Silence.

The soft evening wind blew through Miriam's long dark brunette hair. The sky was lit with warm colors of orange and pink as the sun began to sink behind the rolling hills. The beauty of the surrounding nature was drowned out by the storm that blew in both Miriam's and Joseph's hearts as they both tried to come to terms with the reality of the situation.

Joseph broke the silence, shaking his head and looking at Miriam with pain in his eyes. "This morning I thought that we would be having our wedding tomorrow, and now this! This is a nightmare! I cannot even comprehend what has happened! I have been looking forward to our wedding; I worked extra hard on our home to make it just perfect for you. I thought I knew what tomorrow would bring; now I have no idea of what our future will hold. We will need to speak to the Rabbis tomorrow morning, and they will decide for us what we will do." Joseph wiped the tears from his eyes.

"Tomorrow?" Miriam gasped. If only her secret could have held for one more day. "Oh Joseph ..." she pleaded.

"I love you and hate you right now!" Joseph shook his head sadly. "Come," he sighed, "I must take you back to your father's house. Only God knows what tomorrow holds." He led her by the arm back to her home.

Miriam reluctantly walked back to the house with Joseph. Her worst fears were now realized: she had failed miserably to convince anyone of the truth. All they knew was that she was pregnant. No one believed that she was *supernaturally* pregnant. And there was surely not going to be any wedding for her tomorrow. No one believed her, and she was now pretty convinced that they never would.

Now her only fear was the Rabbis and their decision on whether she deserved to die or if she should live a lifetime of shame.

3 BOLDNESS

Miriam looked out of the window of her room which overlooked the edge of Nazareth and the rolling hill country surrounding the town. Joseph had walked her home to her "prison." Her parents, who were now even more upset, sent her upstairs as soon as she walked through the door. When Joseph left, her family sat down for the evening meal together. Her sister was sent upstairs to bring her a bowl of stew and bread for her to eat alone in her room. She felt humiliated as she sat as prisoner in her own home, eating all by herself.

"Oh God, please don't abandon me now!" Miriam whispered a prayer.

Fear gripped her heart about what might happen tomorrow. As Joseph said, in the morning she would be brought before the Rabbinical Council.

As Miriam stared at the thick stew, she suddenly remembered what the messenger had told her about her cousin, Elizabeth. Elizabeth lived in a small beautiful town in the hills of Jerusalem called Ein Kerem. It was a lovely place with terraces that flourished with grape vines, flowers and olive trees. She was happily married to a Levitical priest named Zachariah. Like most Levites, he served in the Holy Temple in Jerusalem. Throughout their marriage, they were, sadly, never able to conceive children. Almost every other year, when Miriam and her family would travel to Jerusalem for one of the feasts of the Lord, they would stay with them in their home.

Elizabeth was much older than she was, so it was surprising news to Miriam to hear that Elizabeth was pregnant. As Miriam mulled over this, an idea came to her mind. If Elizabeth was pregnant as the angel had said, then maybe this would be some source of refuge for her? For if Elizabeth was exposed to a miracle, then maybe she might consider believing her miracle? Now more than ever, she needed to find someone who might believe her. Plus, she needed to escape. She didn't want to find out what tomorrow would hold if she stayed home. Just the thought of what could happen sent chills up and down her spine. So she decided then and there that, once everyone was asleep, she would begin the daring long journey to Judea to visit her cousin, Elizabeth. It would be taking a chance, but it seemed like a better chance than staying home in Nazareth.

The sound of crickets echoed in the moonlight. Everyone had gone to bed. She could hear the soft rumbles of her Abba snoring from downstairs in his bedroom. Miriam quickly filled a cloth bag with some of her personal items, along with an extra robe and scarf. She looked longingly at the wedding dress that hung in the corner of her room. With a deep sigh she carried on, wrapping a woolen scarf around her hair and face and a thick grey shawl around her shoulders. Then she slowly crept down the stairs. They creaked a little, but thankfully, no one woke up. Down in the kitchen area, she grabbed a loaf of bread and a block of cheese, then snuck out of the house. The door squeaked, but Miriam was careful to shut it quietly. She pulled her shawl in closer around her to keep the cool spring night air from making her feel cold. Miriam opened the front gate of the courtyard, then looked back at her family home. Many happy memories flooded her mind as she looked at the house where she had grown up in all her life. They almost seemed to beckon to her to stay. But then she reminded herself that things were different now. Her whole existence in her own home was at stake. She was now a woman on a mission. With one last loving glance, she blew a silent kiss to her family, then closed the gate behind her.

  Having travelled with her family to Jerusalem almost every other year for one of the

Jewish holidays of Passover, Shavuot, or Feast of Tabernacles, she knew roughly the way or at least the direction towards the hill country of Judea. It would be a long and arduous journey. She would depart from Nazareth traveling towards the east along the Jezreel Valley to the Jordan Valley, then travel south, down along the Jordan Valley along the Jordan River, then make the journey westward past Jericho and Jerusalem, to Ein Kerem. It would be roughly about a 5 - 6-day journey by foot. Maybe if she was lucky, she would be able to hop on a caravan along the way and get there sooner.

    Miriam looked up into the sky and was thankful for the light of the moon to help her see dimly through the darkness. It was very lonely traveling by herself in the dark on the dusty, deserted roads. She hummed to herself out loud to drown out the strange noises, such as the sound of little critters rustling in the bushes along the way. The fear of what tomorrow might hold if she stayed in Nazareth outweighed her fears of traveling alone in the dark. It was risky traveling alone, especially as a young woman. But she was very determined to travel all night in order to create a safe distance between herself and harm's way. She wanted to be as far away from Nazareth as possible before her parents would wake up and discover her absence.

Soon enough the warm morning rays of light stretched across the sky. Exhausted and cold, Miriam knelt down on the rocky edge of the Ein

Harod springs. The spring had special significance, being the place where Gideon and his men drank water before being chosen to stand up against Israel's enemies while being vastly outnumbered.

She cupped her hands and scooped up a long, refreshing drink of the cool, clear water. Her whole body trembled from the long night's journey. Her feet and legs ached. She longed to just lie down under a shady tree somewhere and fall asleep.

There were now other travelers on the road.

"Would you mind helping me fill my jug?" A lady's voice interrupted Miriam's weary daze. She looked up to see a very pretty young lady in an elegant purple robe with intricate needlework standing behind her. Her black hair was also intricately braided and wrapped around like a crown on her head. Her beautiful facial features were augmented with makeup, and an excessive amount of jewelry hung around her ears, neck, and wrists. She held a white clay jug in her hand and reached it out to Miriam to take hold of.

Coming from a humble town, it wasn't common to see such refinery and wealth. Miriam was a bit awe-struck at first. She took the white jug from the wealthy young lady.

"Yes … indeed …" She stumbled over her words, trying not to gawk. She dipped the jug in the water and filled it up. "Here you go." Miriam handed it back to her.

"Thank you, my dear. Where are you from?" she asked.

"From a small village in Lower Galilee," Miriam responded.

"Who are you traveling with?" she asked looking around in search of fellow travelers. She frowned at Miriam. "You are surely not traveling alone?"

"Well … yes, I am on my way to Judea to visit my cousin." Miriam tried not to give away too many details, for fear of word getting out that might reach her family.

"I am not sure if I should congratulate you on your bravery or scold you for being so foolish!" the young lady said, shaking her head. "Come and join our caravan; we are traveling to Jerusalem."

Miriam gasped and stood up with excitement. "Really? I am humbled by your kind offer. Thank you, my dear lady!" she said as she bowed her head graciously.

"Rachel, are you coming?" a man called to the young lady. He too was well dressed, in a fancy white robe with gold trimmings.

"Yes, and I have found another traveler to join us," Rachel replied to the man. She turned to Miriam and gestured for her to follow her to the caravan that was waiting on the road. Miriam couldn't help but gaze at the beautiful purple robe she wore as she followed her. She guessed that they were both around the same age – eighteen years old.

There were three large wooden wagons with canopies made of goat hair canvases covering them, with a set of horses in front of each one. There were also some camels that were part of the caravan. The riders on the camels had swords hanging from their belts. They wore white turbans and looked determined to protect the caravan from any possible danger.

"You may join the wagon that our servants ride in for company," Rachel offered as they drew close to the caravan, "or you may find a place to sleep in the wagon that is holding our luggage and exports."

"I wouldn't mind a rest," Miriam replied, bowing her head humbly. "I am so deeply grateful for this offer!"

A male servant helped Miriam onto the wagon where there was just enough space for her to lie down. The wagon was full of crates and large sacks of food, grains, and spices.

After a while, it lurched forward.

Miriam looked up at the beautiful blue sky above filled with fluffy white clouds. "Thank you, God, for taking care of me," Miriam whispered out loud. Even though she was far away from everything she knew and held dear, she somehow felt safe knowing that her Heavenly Father was watching over her. She leaned down onto the blanket that the male servant had given her, and she quickly fell into a much-needed sleep.

They travelled all day. Miriam stayed mostly in the wagon where she rested. They stopped for lunch along the Jordan River. The servants were friendly and shared some soft pita bread, olives, and creamy sour yogurt. After lunch, the caravan continued along the main road that weaved close to the Jordan River. The Jordan River flowed from the Sea of Galilee in the north and down the Jordan Valley, and into the Salt Sea.

Miriam later learned that the caravan came from Damascus, a city north-east of the Galilee region in the Decapolis, which was also under the Roman Empire. She had heard of Damascus before as being a vibrant city where many merchants and traders flourished. Her father had even travelled there to sell olive oil a couple of times. She soon learned that he man who had called Rachel back to the caravan was her father, who was also a very successful merchant. They continually lived between Damascus and Jerusalem.

As the sun started to dip behind the rugged hills of Samaria, the caravan came to a halt and they set up camp amongst the trees. Other travelers had also set up camp there. Little fires were lit where people were preparing meals of roasted vegetables, stews and meats. The smell made Miriam's stomach grumble. The servants from the caravan busied themselves gathering stones and firewood to build a fire pit, while others began preparations for an evening meal.

"May I help?" Miriam asked one of the older female servants. She had dark, wrinkly weathered skin with white hair tucked under a yellow scarf, and she wore a plain cream colored robe. She looked up at Miriam with a smile and handed her the bowl of dough she was kneading. Miriam rolled up the sleeves of her robe and continued the process of kneading the dough with her hands. Then she and the older lady pulled pieces of the dough out of the bowl and flattened them into round circles and laid them over a metal grill that sat above the fire to bake the flatbread.

Once all the preparations for the meal were complete, Rachel and her father and the guards who had been riding the camels joined the meal. Everyone sat on the ground around the fire to keep warm from the chilly spring evening. They sat on old carpets that the servants had laid out.

"So my curiosity is burning about why a young lady like you would be traveling all by yourself?" Rachel asked as she sat down next to Miriam. Her bangles and necklaces jingled musically as she settled herself comfortably.

"Well," Miriam sighed. She had always been one to share everything easily, which was almost a fault at times. But now she felt very uncomfortable not being able to pour out her heart as she was used to doing in the past. "I am on my way to visit my cousin," she said slowly, choosing her words carefully. "She is married to a priest who serves in the temple. I heard a word that she is pregnant in her old age, so I am going to visit her and hopefully be a help to her." She hoped that she had not said too much.

"That still doesn't explain why you are traveling by yourself," responded Rachel. "I have travelled from Damascus to Jerusalem several times, and I have never seen a girl traveling by herself. You know there are bandits, and you could be kidnapped, raped or robbed?"

"I know it is very dangerous. But I believe that God is looking out for me," Miriam said with a shy smile. "And you have been so kind to me, a true gift from above."

Rachel leaned in and whispered into Miriam's ear, "You are running away. Why?"

"How do you know?" Miriam blurted out in surprise.

"It's the only thing that makes sense." Rachel nodded her head for Miriam to tell all.
"I promise not to tell."

"I'm really bad at keeping things in," Miriam sighed. "It's a fault of mine."

"Go on and tell me," Rachel prodded. "I told you I won't tell."

"Well, you're not going to believe my story. No one has believed me. Sometimes I even wonder myself if it is true," Miriam began.

"Why wouldn't I believe you?"

Miriam hesitated. "You see I am betrothed … or *was* … betrothed … to a wonderful carpenter," Miriam said wistfully. "During our betrothal, I had a special visitor … an angel." Miriam looked at Rachel closely to see if she was following.

Rachel furrowed her brow. "An *angel?*" she asked, cocking her head to the side.

"Not many people have seen angels, they are special messengers from heaven that God sends to give a message. Do you remember the stories from the Tanach? It's not common, but it has happened before."

"I've heard some of the stories; my family is not so religious. But yes, I do recall hearing about angels and that they often came to give a message. Did he have a special message for you?" Rachel asked.

"Well ... yes," Miriam hesitated again. "You're very good at asking questions!"

Rachel smiled. "It's true. That's how I get what I want," she smirked. "So what happened?" she prodded.

"One day I was at home, by myself, cleaning the house when the angel came to visit. And in short, he said that I . . . that I would conceive and give birth to our Messiah, the Messiah of Israel."

Rachel's eyebrows shot up. "You would be the mother of the Messiah?" she asked in disbelief.

"Yes, to the Son of David," Miriam said.

"Interesting. If what you are saying is true, I am very surprised, because I figured the Messiah would never come. Our people have gone through so much chaos, why wouldn't the Messiah not come at those times? My father says that God is angry with us because we have never been good at following God's Commandments – that are impossible to keep anyway – and that is why our people have been expelled and persecuted so many times. God is mad at us, I guess, or has completely forsaken us."

"Of course the Messiah is coming. The prophets have spoken about Him," Miriam insisted as she shook her head.

"So tell me what happened," Rachel said, returning Miriam to the story.

"So I guess … I became pregnant without ever sleeping with a man," Miriam sighed, shrugging her shoulders.

"Are you *serious?*" Rachel laughed out loud.

Miriam nodded.

"What did your betrothed say to this?"

"He didn't believe me, nor did my family. They think I slept with someone." Miriam looked down at her sandaled feet and sighed. "In the morning, they were going to bring me before the Rabbinical Council, and coming from a very traditional town I know they would not deal lightly with my situation." She shuddered at the thought of any of the possible outcomes that could be imagined.

"Well, it is a bit hard to believe that you can become pregnant without knowing a man!" Rachel stated.

"I know … but I have," Miriam shrugged.

"Well, I don't know …" Rachel shrugged her shoulders. "For one, I'm not even sure there will ever be a Messiah. What will he do? Save us from Rome? Will he become like the Pharisees? They are probably the closest to God, but to be honest, I am afraid of them. They are overly condemning and judgmental, I think. I feel uncomfortable when I am around them. And they don't even seem happy. Who would want to live such a life?"

Miriam assumed that Rachel came from the Sadducee denomination of thought amongst the Jewish people, those who adapted themselves to the hellenistic culture while maintaining their faith in the God of Israel. And for herself, in Nazareth, the village delved more towards the Pharisaic school of thought, which was a more stringent lifestyle of overzealous observance of the torah.

"Well, surely He will restore the Kingdom of Israel," Miriam said. "And He will lead our people like King David."

"I hope so," Rachel said doubtfully.

"He is coming to save us!" Miriam declared confidently.

The conversation was then interrupted by Rachel's father who picked up an oud, and some of the male guards pulled out some drums with leather skins stretched over the top, while one of the servants pulled out a flute, and a whole music session began. Other travelers in the area slowly began to join in the music, whether it was pulling out their own instruments or clapping or singing along. Miriam began to sway to the beat of the music. Rachel pulled out her tambourine and began dancing around the fire. At one point, she put down her tambourine and pulled Miriam to her feet, and soon both girls were dancing together. For a moment, Miriam forgot all about her troubles as she whirled and twirled around with Rachel to the lively melodies.

4 A HOME

Miriam stood at the gate of Zachariah and Elizabeth's home. She took hold of the cord that hung from the bell by the gate of the courtyard that led to the house. Before ringing it, she paused. This was the moment of truth. The angel had told Miriam that Elizabeth, who was advanced in age, would also be pregnant. Elizabeth had been barren throughout her whole marriage, and it would be an incredible miracle that at her age she could suddenly conceive a baby. If what the angel had said was true, and Elizabeth was really pregnant, then she would have no doubt in her mind that she was also carrying the future Messiah for the people of Israel. And hopefully, since they had supposedly received a miracle baby, they could also believe that she was also carrying a baby by supernatural means.

      She pulled the cord to ring the bell. It clanged loud and clear for those in the house to hear. Miriam peered through the gate. Soon, the wooden door of the house swung open. She saw an elderly woman with soft silvery hair pulled back in a thick braid waddling her way towards her with a large belly. It was Elizabeth! Miriam gasped as she could clearly see an undeniable, very large, very pregnant belly. It was an incredible sight. Elizabeth was indeed pregnant!

Miriam nearly started jumping with joy! "Elizabeth!" she called from behind the gate. "It's me, Miriam, daughter of Heli!"

"Miriam?" Elizabeth exclaimed with disbelief. Her blue eyes widened with surprise. She pulled open the gate and quickly embraced her cousin.

"Oh Elizabeth, God bless you!" Miriam shouted in amazement. "It is true!" She then stood back and looked at Elizabeth, who beamed happily at her surprise guest. Miriam gently touched Elizabeth's belly.

"The baby just leapt in my womb!" Elizabeth exclaimed, grasping her belly at the sudden movement within. She looked up at Miriam with her blue eyes beaming. "Blessed are you among women, and blessed is the fruit of your womb! The mother of our Messiah!" the words suddenly blurted from her mouth. They both looked at each other in shock and disbelief!

"What did you just say?" Miriam could hardly get the words out of her own mouth as her ears rung from Elizabeth's words. Since the visitation from the angel and discovering she was supernaturally pregnant, it had been a difficult time of doubt, shame and fear. From trying to convince those close to her that she was to be the mother of the Messiah, then to trying to hide it, and then having to make the gutsy escape from her little town, how could it be that suddenly, without saying a word, without having to convince anyone, that she would just know? Not knowing what to say or how to respond, Miriam's big brown eyes filled with tears and she just began to weep.

Elizabeth lovingly embraced the brave young traveler. "Now, now, my dear, come inside and find rest." She led her into her home. One of her handmaidens greeted them at the door.

"Please, take Miriam and help her freshen up. The poor dear has come a long way and is with child," Elizabeth kindly requested of her handmaiden. The young handmaiden bowed her head respectfully and then took Miriam aside where she was able to help her wash away all of the dust from the long journey from Nazareth to En Kerem. She handed her a fresh, clean, cream-colored robe and a brown cotton tunic with some beautiful stitching along the edges. Then she brushed her hair and braided it.

Miriam stepped outside on the terrace, where Elizabeth was resting on some pillows.

"You look beautiful, my dear!" Elizabeth greeted her. She patted the pillow next to her for

Miriam to come and join her. The terrace was nicely shaded by wooden beams above that were covered with vines and flowers.

Miriam felt a whole lot better after freshening up. "Thank you, Elizabeth, for your kind hospitality," she said as she sat down next to her. "I appreciate your kindness to me!"

"So why is it granted to me, that the mother of my Messiah should come to me?" Elizabeth asked with a smile.

Miriam smiled back; her heart skipped a beat. *She said it again!* It felt surreal that Elizabeth believed the truth of what God had spoken to her, and that she was being honored by her as well.

"The baby leaped for joy in my womb as your greeting sounded in my ears!" Elizabeth caressed her large tummy.

"This feels like a dream!" Miriam exclaimed excitedly. She then told Elizabeth all about the recent events.

Elizabeth listened intently to the whole story. "Blessed is she who believed, for there will be a fulfilment of those things which were told her from the Lord," she said confidently.

Miriam suddenly stood up and began pacing back and forth on the terrace, her heart stirred up within. For too long she had felt suppressed by doubt and shame. Now it was time to rejoice! Now she was free! "My soul magnifies the Lord, and my spirit has rejoiced in God my Savior. For He has regarded the lowly state of His maidservant; for henceforth all generations will call me blessed. For He who is mighty has done great things for me, and holy is His Name. And His mercy is on those who fear Him from generation to generation. He has shown strength with His arm; He has scattered the proud in the imagination of their hearts. He has put down the mighty from their thrones and exalted the lowly. He has filled the hungry with good things, and the rich He has sent away empty. He has helped His servant Israel, in remembrance of His mercy, as he spoke to our fathers, to Abraham, and to His seed forever," Miriam proclaimed.

"Amen and amen, my dear," Elizabeth nodded her head. "God has not forsaken us His people."

That evening, Zachariah came home and was pleasantly surprised to see Miriam in his home. A big smile spread across his face, and he gave Miriam a kiss on each cheek. Miriam was very excited to see Zachariah. He was a famous storyteller in her family. Throughout her life, whenever they stayed over at Zachariah and Elizabeth's house, they always looked forward to hearing his stories. He was a no-nonsense type of fellow with a strong, sarcastic kind of humor. Miriam loved listening to his stories, his witty remarks and comic way of expressing himself which often had Miriam and her whole family roaring with laughter.

"Adoni!" Miriam greeted him excitedly. To her surprise, he didn't say a word in return, but just simply smiled back at her.

"Zachariah? It's me, Miriam!" she said while looking at him curiously.

He shrugged his shoulders, and with his hands, he tried to communicate something to her with hand gestures.

Miriam was very confused. She looked at Elizabeth.

"Oh Miriam, I forgot to mention that Zachariah is mute now," she explained. "He has been mute ever since he left the temple for his services, right before I became pregnant."

"Oh, I am sorry to hear that," Miriam said with disappointment. She then turned back to face Zachariah and started making hand movements to try to express her joy at being in their home. Zachariah waved his hands and then pointed to his ears. Elizabeth laughed.

"He can still hear, my dear; he's not deaf," Elizabeth said. "Come now, let's sit down for dinner, and I want you to share the whole story with Zachariah." They sat down on some pillows along a low table. The handmaiden who had helped Miriam freshen up from her long journey set out a lovely meal before them. They had lentil stew, tomato and cucumber salad all chopped up into little pieces with olive oil and lemon juice all tossed together, and some fresh bread on the side.

Miriam once again recounted the whole story.

Zachariah listened intently and nodded the whole time. When Miriam spoke about the angel, his eyes suddenly grew wide. He pounded his chest and pointed to himself.

"What, Zachariah?" Elizabeth asked.

He turned to Elizabeth, and he pointed to his eyes.

"You also saw the angel?" she asked in disbelief. After several months of Zachariah being mute, she understood his sign language very well.

Zachariah nodded.

"Was it the same one?" Elizabeth asked Miriam.

"He was tall with a perfectly white robe, and he had a radiant complexion. I think he must have looked like Moses when he came down from the mountain of Sinai. He had a very comforting presence." Miriam tried to describe the messenger. Zachariah nodded his head profusely. He pointed up to the sky and then pointed to Elizabeth's stomach.

"The angel told you that we were going to have our baby?" Elizabeth asked.

Zachariah nodded. Miriam could see that his eyes were beginning to water. Once again he pointed up, then made his hand talk, then pointed to himself and then looked at Elizabeth. He put his hand gently on her tummy, then with his other hand pointed to Miriam's belly.

"The angel told you about our baby? And he told you about Miriam's baby?" Elizabeth tried to make sense of Zachariah's hand gestures. He rolled his hands around to gesture for more.

"Our babies are connected somehow?" Elizabeth asked.

Zachariah nodded and began to weep, rocking back and forth, lifting his arms high.

Miriam's arms tightened with goosebumps.

Elizabeth looked at her, and they both began to weep. Despite all the woes, there was a sense that something bigger and more important than themselves was orchestrating something beyond them.

Miriam continued the rest of her story of how none of her family believed her, how Joseph didn't believe, and how she had to run away from home.

"Miriam, it is so good that you are here," Elizabeth said and then looked at Zachariah and continued. "Please, our home is your home, and you are free to stay here for the rest of your life if need be."

Zachariah nodded in agreement.

"I am grateful beyond measure!" Miriam bowed humbly. "Thank you for your kindness to me!"

Elizabeth reached out and grasped her hand. "Consider this your home from now on."

That night as Miriam laid in bed, she marveled at everything that had transpired since her arrival. She had found more than a refuge; she found a new home for herself. Elizabeth and Zachariah had gone so far as to offer her a place to live for the rest of her life. She hadn't really thought about life beyond the pregnancy. But it would be true, if Joseph was no longer in the picture, then she would have to raise the Messiah by herself and would probably never be married as a result of having a baby out of wedlock.

Her life had taken on a whole new twist. No longer would she be able to think about being Joseph's wife or raising a family together, or growing old together with him. That was now a closed chapter. Miriam tried not to feel disheartened over this matter, but she couldn't help but long for Joseph, whom she missed terribly.

Being chosen to be the mother of the Son of God was not without sacrifice.

5 THE LAMB

A couple weeks passed since Miriam had taken refuge with Zachariah and Elizabeth in their home in En Keren, a small town outside of Jerusalem. They warmly took her in as their own. Miriam did her best to be helpful around the house, especially since Elizabeth was full-term and would soon be delivering her miracle baby. She helped with cooking the meals, cleaning around the house, the laundry, and doing errands for the family. Miriam herself was feeling stronger and ideally better, as she was now past the third month of her pregnancy.

She sat on a stool in the kitchen and gently scratched the scruffy nose of a little lamb that was in the house. It was to be their Passover lamb. Miriam always had mixed feelings about this time of the year, as it was often too easy to fall in love with the Passover lamb who, according to tradition, would live in the house with them for three days, and then, on the day of Passover, would be taken to the Temple where it was to be sacrificed, and its blood poured at the foot of the altar as an atonement. Then the man of the house would bring the slaughtered lamb home where they would roast it for dinner as commanded. They would have to consume the whole lamb by midnight, as was directed in the Torah.

Today, according to the Jewish calendar, it was Nisan 14, which meant that it was the day of Passover. As was written in the law of Moses, all the men were asked to assemble in Jerusalem to present a lamb sacrifice. Thousands of Jewish families or representatives of each family were gathered there as a result. There was a lot of celebrations taking place and many travelers filled the streets of the city and the surrounding towns, including En Kerem.

Miriam was at first worried that her family might show up in Jerusalem or even come and stay with Zachariah and Elizabeth, as they sometimes did for Passover in the past. But Zachariah made sure that his house was filled with relatives from his side of the family this time. Miriam was very cautious when she ventured out of the house in case she might bump into anyone she knew from Nazareth.

Zachariah came into the room and smiled at Miriam. She smiled back and then bent down by the little lamb.

"Bye, cutie!" She kissed the lamb goodbye on its head.

Zachariah tied a rope around the lamb's neck, creating a collar and leash to make it easy for traveling. He made some hand gestures to Miriam.

"Why don't you go with him to Jerusalem, my dear?" Elizabeth asked, reading the gestures for Miriam.

"I really want to," Miriam hesitated, "but I'm just afraid of bumping into someone from Nazareth."

"There are thousands upon thousands of people in Jerusalem right now," said Elizabeth. "It would be difficult to bump into someone from Nazareth ... Here, take this scarf and wrap it around your face." Elizabeth took a simple, beige-colored scarf and wrapped it around Miriam's head and then covered the bottom of her face with it.

"Thank you, Elizabeth," said Miriam as she hugged her. "I really do want to go!"

Zachariah and Miriam headed out of town on the upward journey to Jerusalem. It was about a two-hour walk, with no stops. The rocky road was filled with travelers on their way to Jerusalem. Miriam followed in Zachariah's footsteps.

Soon, she could see Jerusalem in the distance, with the Holy Temple standing tall and magnificent on top. Miriam grew excited as they got closer. And as they got closer, the crowd grew denser and noisier. Soon enough Miriam was shoulder to shoulder with other travelers as she followed Zachariah and the lamb into the city of Jerusalem. Music and singing filled the streets; children were playing and running around, while old men with canes watched with pride. The bleating of lambs joined in the melody of the crowds. Money changers and merchants stood along the sides of the streets, trying to get people's attention. The air was electric with joy and celebrations. Miriam carefully scanned the crowd to make sure she didn't see anyone she recognized, and carefully held the scarf over her face, so only her big brown eyes were exposed.

    They entered through one of the gates of Jerusalem and joined the long line up to the mikvah where they would both have to immerse themselves in water before going up to the Temple. Zachariah went into the line with the men, while Miriam entered the line with the women. Miriam couldn't wait to enter the temple courts and be among the worshippers and musicians. She loved the thought of being closer to the presence of God, who dwelt in the Holy of Holies in the inner court of the Temple. Miriam secretly wished that she could enter that place, to experience what it would be like to be in the most sacred place where His presence dwelt, with no curtain or courts to separate her from God. However, only the High Priests were able to enter the Holy of Holies, and even so, one had to be careful. Miriam remembered hearing the story of how Moses and the priests were unable to stand in His presence. And there was also a Psalm of David where he uttered the words, "Better to be a doorkeeper in the house of the Lord than anywhere else." He must have been in the Holy of Holies in the tabernacle, Miriam mused. She had been at the temple before and had felt the warmth of being close to God's presence. It made her feel whole inside, feeding the yearning of the deepest inner part of her heart. There was nothing like it in the whole world …

Then, she looked down at her belly and placed her hand on it. Her mind tried to comprehend how God Divine could be within her womb! She knew He was in the Temple in the inner courts, dwelling between the cherubim on the Ark of the Covenant, and now, He was within her! How could this be? she wondered …

When it was her turn to enter the mikva, someone was there to hold her belongings. She stripped down to her undergarments and then walked down the stone steps into a pool of cool running water. She fully immersed herself under the water and then turned around and walked up the steps and out as someone else walked down in after her.

The attendee handed Miriam her robe, tunic and scarf. She did her best to wring out the water from her undergarments, then pulled her robe over herself and her tunic on. After she had finished dressing, she was just about to go through the door to leave the mikva and look for Zachariah.

"Miriam!"

She heard someone call her name. Startled, she whirled around to see who it might be.

A young lady with a beautiful purple robe stood behind her; she was also damp from the mikva. Her black eyeliner smeared a little from the water. It was Rachel!

Miriam breathed a sigh of relief.

"Happy holidays, my dear!" Rachel greeted Miriam with a kiss on the cheek.

Miriam curtsied, and with a sense of relief, embraced her. "Oh, so glad it's you!" she sighed.

"Are you all by yourself again?" Rachel asked, half-teasing and half-scolding. "Don't tell me you're still on the run?"

"No, I am here with my older cousin Zachariah to bring our Passover lamb to the Temple."

"Good girl!" Rachel teased.

Miriam changed the subject. "You know, I am so grateful that you picked me up like an orphan along the road."

"It was nothing." Rachel waved her hand. "Don't mention it." She looked down at Miriam's belly. "This is incredible." she placed her hand on Miriam's stomach and caressed it gently. "I've been thinking about you and about your story which … I hope is true. And if you are the mother of our Messiah, I would like to give this to you." She removed her deep royal blue silk scarf with intricate white flowers and Stars of David embroidered into the fabric along the edges. She then wrapped it around Miriam's shoulders.

Miriam gasped in surprise. She ran her fingers over the smooth, expensive material.
"This is too much!" she exclaimed. She removed the beige wool scarf and put on the blue scarf over her hair.

"Don't say anything. Be blessed!" Rachel laughed and gave Miriam a goodbye kiss on her cheek and then she left with her entourage of maidservants.

Miriam walked out of the mikva, still admiring the beautiful scarf. She looked up and saw Zachariah waiting for her by the bottom of the Temple steps. He nodded his head in approval of the beautiful new scarf.

"Zachariah, I've never owned anything so beautiful!" Miriam exclaimed. "I just bumped into Rachel, the one who invited me to join their caravan to Jerusalem from Ein Harod. Isn't it gorgeous?"

Zachariah gave Miriam a pat on her back to express his approval. Then together they went through the Huldah Gate and began the ascent up the limestone stairs of the Temple. It was a long ascent of about 3 stories high. Zachariah helped Miriam up the stairs by linking arms with her, while carrying the lamb around his shoulders.

As they walked up the steps to the Temple, Miriam noticed the blood of the lambs stained on the stairs as people carried away their slaughtered lambs. She glanced over at their Passover lamb around Zachariah's shoulders with a feeling of sadness. The custom of sacrificing Passover lambs began hundreds of years ago when her people were in Egypt under the bondage of slavery. The day before her people were set free, Moses had told each Israelite family to slaughter a lamb, and dip the blood in hyssop and stain the doorposts of their home with the blood of the lamb so that the angel of death would pass over them. Miriam wondered how the blood of animals was useful to God for saving them.

As they reached the top step to the Temple, they walked into the Court of the Gentiles, which was an area where both Jews and non-Jews alike could be together. It was more like a bazaar where people could purchase an animal sacrifice, souvenirs, spices from the Far East, painted pottery pieces, ornate clay lamps, and many more items. And there were also money changers where people were made to change their money from Roman coins to Tyrian money because the Jewish leaders felt that the Roman money was not pure and thus needed to be exchanged to a "purer" currency.

They walked around the stalls for a few minutes, then Zachariah gestured for Miriam to follow him through the 'Beautiful Gate', where only Jewish men and women were allowed to enter. Then all the men with the animal sacrifices went through the Nicanor Gate where the sacrifices would take place. Miriam stayed behind in the Women's Court. Singing broke out, and Miriam joined in with the singing and worshipping God. She closed her eyes as she sang with all her might. She felt weary from the long trip and the many stairs they had just climbed, but her soul had longed for this moment where she could be ever closer to God, to be close to His presence. Her thoughts drifted far from her sore feet. She could feel the holy presence of the Almighty fill her soul afresh. It felt like fresh, clean water being poured upon her thirsty soul.

"Dear God, help me to be strong and be a good mother to the Messiah," Miriam whispered a prayer from her heart.

Time went by quickly, and soon Zachariah returned with the slaughtered lamb, and together they began the descent from the Temple. With her soul feeling refreshed, she felt like she was dancing down the steps.

Then suddenly, as they were leaving the Huldah Gate, out of the corner of her eye Miriam saw a group of Roman soldiers who were standing, drinking water and noshing on some fresh pita. She looked away quickly and lifted up the scarf over her face and then glanced again. Indeed, one of the Roman soldiers was very familiar to her from her hometown of Nazareth. Their eyes suddenly met. Miriam quickly looked away. She had never spoken to him before, but had seen him several times in the marketplace or riding his horse around the town. One time he had even come to her family's home demanding taxes for Rome. She almost felt tempted to go up to him and ask him about her family and about Joseph, but then, she was afraid that if he were to return to Nazareth, he would reveal her whereabouts. Who knows what Joseph intended for her.

Before she could decide, the Roman soldier looked back at her and then began to approach her. "The most beautiful runaway bride of the north!" he bellowed loudly with a sneer.

Miriam blushed.

"Was it a big bad fight? Or are you a bad cook or something, that he would decide to divorce a pretty face like yours? If you don't come back quick, he may marry someone else, you know. Word has it that he is now interested in taking one of the wine dresser's daughters as his wife," he laughed. "Or perhaps Joseph is a wise man not to take a wife that gallivants around on her own. You should have stayed in the kitchen where you belong, you little Jewess!"

"This is none of your business!" Miriam retorted, she felt humiliated and turned around to leave. Her heart began to beat wildly. How dare he! How dare he mock her in public! Suddenly, she felt she had more to say, and before she could make up her mind on whether to hold her tongue or not, she swung around to face him again. "Right now," she burst out, "I am carrying the Messiah of Israel who will redeem our people from Rome's tyranny!"

The Roman soldier looked stunned by her boldness. "Careful, little lady, I wouldn't defy

Rome if I were you!" he half-laughed and half-warned.

Zachariah pulled on Miriam's arm for them to leave.

Miriam glared back at the soldier who was staring at her as he stuffed more pita into his mouth. She scowled at him, then joined Zachariah in the descent down the stairs.

Her heart now felt heavy as her mind swirled with questions. The thought of Joseph loving someone else saddened her. Would he bring his new wife into the house that Joseph had built for her? Would he smile at her as he smiled at her? Would he caress her hair as he caressed hers? She shook her head. She couldn't let her mind run any further in that direction, or it would drive her heart mad. Losing Joseph was by far the biggest sacrifice she could ever make in her lifetime. And she was convinced that it would be impossible for her to love another person like she had loved him. Miriam remembered the moment she first laid eyes on him; it was love at first sight! And never before had she felt that way about anyone. He was so handsome, with gorgeous brown eyes; he was tall, muscular, and most of all, kind and generous. He had the best smile, and his eyes were full of life and love. When she was first getting to know him, she would feel awkward around him and could hardly even speak straight. But then, little by little, a special friendship grew between them, and much to Miriam's delight, he requested her hand in marriage! She had felt like the luckiest girl in the world to have found favor in his eyes. From that moment, her future and her every thought had become wrapped around him; all her dreams and hopes were connected to him. And now ... that was all taken away. Letting go was not easy for her young heart. Even though she esteemed the God of her people over her beloved Joseph, it was still a hard process to let go.

Her love for God grew from her constant curiosity, starting from a young girl; she loved going to the synagogue and listening to the Rabbis read from the Tanach and sometimes she would even eavesdrop on the lessons they taught the boys in the village. Her father was also a wonderful storyteller and would share stories from the Bible, tales of interesting people, history of her people, lessons about life, etc. He was an endless well of knowledge. And Miriam would soak it all in. She especially loved the stories about the heroes of Israel and about the soon-coming Messiah. For too long they had been plundered over and over again. For that reason, from a very tender age, she, along with her people, Israel, longed for the Messiah. And now that she was given the high calling to mother the Messiah, how could she deny her people, even though it meant losing the closest thing to her heart, Joseph? Miriam mulled over her thoughts the whole journey back to En Kerem.

When Miriam and Zachariah returned back to the house, they began the preparations for the Passover meal.

"My dear, you are very quiet, is everything alright?" Elizabeth asked as she slowly inched her way slowly into the kitchen to get a drink of water out of the pitcher. She looked very uncomfortable carrying the weight of the growing child within her.

"I saw someone I recognized from Nazareth today," Miriam said quietly. "… He recognized me."

"Oh no!" Elizabeth exclaimed.

"It was a Roman soldier, and he told me that Joseph might marry someone else," Miriam sighed. "I think I still love him, Elizabeth. I know it's over, but it made me so sad to hear this news."

"You are the most blessed woman to be the mother of the Messiah," Elizabeth said trying to encourage her.

"I have nothing to complain about," Miriam sighed. "I just wish my heart and emotions would understand this."

6 MAKE WAY

Miriam brought in the washing from outside where it had been hanging to dry, and she began to fold the items in the bedroom.

She suddenly heard a loud groan from Elizabeth. She dropped the tunic she was folding and ran into the kitchen to Elizabeth's side. Elizabeth groaned again, and her face suddenly contorted. "Oh, my Lord! I keep getting tight around my abdomen … I'm not sure if it's time, or if it's just the preparations for the …" She groaned a third time. Then, suddenly, her waters broke, drenching the bottom of her robe, her legs, and her leather-sandaled feet. Elizabeth and Miriam looked at each other in disbelief.

"It's time!" Elizabeth exclaimed.
"Zachariah!" Miriam shouted.
Zachariah ran into the kitchen.
"It's time! Please get the midwife!"

Zachariah nodded and quickly ran out of the house.

Miriam led Elizabeth to the bedroom and helped her onto the bed.

Elizabeth moaned and groaned at each contraction. "I'm too old for this!" she said, wiping her sweaty brow.

Soon, the midwife arrived, and Miriam did whatever she bid her to do.

After several hours of labor, and when the moon had risen high in the sky, the baby was at last born.

Elizabeth held her new baby boy in her arms and beamed with motherly pride. "Oh, how I have longed for this day … to be a mother!" Elizabeth rejoiced as she gently caressed her son's little sweet face.

Zachariah came into the room. He gestured *excitement* with his arms and silently blessed the baby and Elizabeth. Miriam watched as the new mother and father doted on their dear baby boy. The fresh new life was greeted with the adoring love of his parents.

Through the evening and throughout the week, many visitors came to visit and congratulate the new parents. The whole neighborhood was brimming with excitement and had to come to see the new baby. They were all amazed that Elizabeth was, at last, a mother in her old age! It was truly a miracle, and each visitor rejoiced with them!

As was the custom for every Jewish boy, on the eighth day many friends and relatives gathered for the circumcision ceremony of the baby. Also on this day, it was customary to announce to everyone the name of the baby.

"So you will name him Zachariah of course?" one of the neighbors smiled.

"Actually no," Elizabeth answered, to his surprise.

The whole room quieted down.

"His name is John."

They were not prepared for Elizabeth's answer. It was the tradition for the oldest son in a family to take on the name of the father or a close relative.

"Is the name John in your family?" a neighbor lady asked.

Some of the guests turned to Zachariah to see if he was agreeable to this.

"Give him a writing tablet," suggested another lady, "and let's see what name he writes down!"

They handed him a writing tablet. Zachariah grasped it and wrote: *"His name is John."*

Everyone gasped with surprise.

Suddenly, Zachariah stood up and, to everyone's astonishment, he began to speak.

"Friends and family, praise be to God of Israel! Yes, his name is John. An angel of the Lord appeared to me and told me to name him John. He will be a

Nazarene, one who abstains from wine or strong drink and will be filled with the Holy Spirit. He will go before the Messiah in the spirit of Elijah to turn the hearts of the children to the father; to make ready a people prepared for the Lord," Zachariah declared zealously.

Everyone was in awe.

"What kind of child will this be?" someone asked.

"For this child to be born during the week of Passover is very significant," said another person.

Meanwhile, Miriam was taking all of this in. She felt goosebumps while Zachariah proclaimed John's name. The hope in her heart for her people and the whole nation of Israel was growing stronger. Surely God was with them and had not forgotten them. She looked out the window to the deep blue sky above. Not only did she feel that God had not forgotten His people, but He had not forgotten her, and had made way for her not to be alone. She placed her hands on her expanding belly. "Just wait, little one," she whispered. "You will not be alone. John will help prepare the way for you."

The weeks went by quickly. Early one evening, Miriam was just waking up from a nap. It had been a warm day, and feeling tired, she had gone to her room to catch up on some rest. As she slowly roused herself out of her slumber, she could hear people talking in the house. She yawned and stretched as she sat up on the bed. She tried to listen to the voices and decipher what they were saying. She could hear Elizabeth speaking rather excitedly. Miriam was curious to know who else was there, so she slowly maneuvered off the bed and stood up to see what the commotion was about. As she cracked the door of her room open to peek through, she could see Elizabeth rocking little baby John in her arms, Zachariah standing next to her.

Then she saw the back of a tall young man. Her heart began to race. Right away, she recognized who it was. She quickly closed the door. Was she just imagining things? Questions began to swirl around in her mind. How did he find her? Had he come to bring her home to Nazareth to present her before the Rabbinical council in the town? Why else would he be here?

She opened the door again to make sure she wasn't mistaken. It was indeed him! Somehow word must have reached Nazareth that she was with Zachariah and Elizabeth. But who would have told him? Surely not the Roman soldier! Whatever the case, she decided that she wasn't going to wait to figure out this mystery. Instead, she needed to get away before he found her. She had escaped before, and she could do it again. Miriam looked around the room for a way out. There was a tiny window. She looked down at her expanded belly. She sighed. She would never be able to fit through at this rate. There was no way to escape from the house, except by sneaking out.

She cracked open the door a third time. She slowly opened it wider and then wider, while they continued to talk, not noticing the door opening up. She carefully slipped through the opening, which was just wide enough for her and her belly bump to sneak through. Escaping was much easier before her belly had expanded. Her heart beat so loud, she was almost afraid that it would blow her cover. She carefully maneuvered down the hall against the wall. She made it successfully to the back door without being detected. Then, with a rush of adrenaline, she nearly leaped out the door. But as she exited the door, her robe caught on one of the clay pots that stood at the entrance of the door and dragged it to the ground, smashing it to little pieces on the floor.

The crashing noise caught everyone's attention.

Miriam continued to run out the back door, across the terrace and to the garden. There was no time to hesitate!

"Miriam! Stop!"

She could hear Elizabeth and Zachariah shouting behind her, but she continued to run and run. She could hear the footsteps of someone at her heels. She glanced back and saw . . . Joseph! It startled her and caused her to lose her footing, and she began to fall forward. Joseph quickly caught her in his arms.

"No! Save me!" she shouted. "Help me!" She looked at Joseph, who struggled to hold her in his arms. "You don't understand! If you only knew the truth!"

"I *do* know the truth!" Joseph held her strongly as she struggled against his grip.

"No, you don't!" Miriam continued her struggle to free herself, trying to ignore his handsome good looks. "God has chosen me!"

"I believe you, Miriam," Joseph said calmly.

Miriam suddenly stopped. She looked at Joseph in shock. Their eyes met. He looked at her with concern in his eyes. There was no anger and pain in his eyes like their last encounter.

"What?" Miriam asked, dumbfounded. "What do you mean?"

"Miriam, I believe you!" Joseph said again.

"You believe me?"

She looked over at Zachariah and Elizabeth who were standing by the back door of the house. They smiled at her.

"No, you don't!" she began to struggle again. "You called me a whore!"

"I know, and I am sorry. Please, hear me out!" Joseph pinned her arms down. "I have much to tell you, but first, I must say that I am so glad to have found you! I have searched high and low for you!" He then pulled her close to him in an embrace and planted a kiss on her head. He held her tight as if he never wanted to let her go.

Miriam felt disoriented and confused. She never imagined that Joseph would ever hold her again, let alone kiss her on her forehead! Miriam touched the spot where he had kissed her. "Joseph … I thought … I mean, how do you believe me?" *Could he still love her?* she wondered.

They sat down on the wooden bench in the garden, Joseph still holding her close to him.

"Thank God you are alive and well!" Joseph caressed her hair. "And I have been so worried about you!"

Suddenly, Miriam started to feel a little impatient and annoyed. She was very confused by the way he was caressing her. She stood up quickly. "Joseph, what is going on here? Why are you …? How is it that you say you believe me? You were going to send me to the Sanhedrin where they probably would have stoned me to death! Is this a trick to bring me home so they can still stone me?"

"No! Of course not!" Joseph stood up next to her. "Miriam, I have been searching for you and have been trying to find you ever since you disappeared. I am just so relieved to see you again. I have been worried sick about you! Now," he begged her, "please sit down and let me explain."

She sat down next to Joseph to listen to what he had to say.

"So, it went like this. After our last encounter, I had gone home deeply upset, as you know. Never before had I been so angry, and I felt deeply betrayed. But never mind about that. I am so sorry about how I spoke to you. So, that night, I couldn't sleep at all … I was a complete mess. I couldn't bear the thought of you getting hurt, even though I was convinced that you had slept with someone else. But I was also worried the Sanhedrin would come to an awful decision, of perhaps stoning, for example. So I finally concluded that I would just divorce you quietly, so you wouldn't become a public example. Even after I had come to this decision, I continued to toss and turn in bed, and eventually I fell asleep.

"Now comes the most interesting part … While I was sleeping, I had a special dream from God. Never have I ever had a dream like this. God spoke to me. He said, 'Joseph, Son of David, do not be afraid to take Miriam as your wife, for that which is conceived in her is of the Holy Spirit.' Just like you said. He said that you would bring forth a Son and we shall call Him Yeshua, for He will save His people from their sins."

Miriam was astonished. She couldn't believe her ears! She looked up to heaven and clapped her hands. "How can this be!" she asked in disbelief. "God spoke to you too!"

"Yes of course," Joseph exclaimed. "And that is why we are going to be married, and together, we shall raise the Messiah!"

Miriam shook her head in amazement as a big smile spread across her face. She felt like crying and laughing all at the same time. Her heart was even more jubilant than the night he first asked for her hand in marriage from her father. She threw her arms around his neck.

"This is a gift from God!" she sobbed, through tears and smiles.

"The biggest and most humbling gift," Joseph concurred. "So the story continues, that when I woke up from the dream, I went straight away to your house to meet your father to tell him my dream. But when I arrived at your family's home, they were all in a fury. Your sister Hannah had gone up to your room to bring you some breakfast and discovered you were gone. We then searched the whole village the first couple of days; then we searched the hills and orchards and surrounding area for weeks. We looked in caves to see if you had found refuge somewhere. We had no idea that you would make this long journey as a young woman all by yourself to En Kerem. It didn't even enter our minds. We searched the surrounding villages, and we kept on hearing the same thing over and over again, that no one had seen you or even heard about you. We assumed you were hiding somewhere. Or worst of all, I was afraid that maybe you had encountered a wild animal ... but I also couldn't believe that God would allow that to happen to you while you were pregnant with the Son of God! I knew that God was taking care of you. Thus finally, we decided to wait it out, hoping that you would eventually come out of hiding.

"Then about a couple weeks ago, I was in Tiberias delivering some furniture, when one of the Roman centurions who had been stationed in our area approached me. He said he had seen you in

Jerusalem. Right away, I told your father the news, and he said that you must have gone to be with your relatives here, so I have been searching amongst Jerusalem and the surrounding towns until I finally came here to En Kerem …" Joseph smiled. "And here you are!"

"The Roman soldier! He recognized me and laughed at me!" Miriam exclaimed. "He told me that you were thinking of marrying one of the wine dresser's daughters!"

"Always interesting how people come up with these conclusions. But as you know, our village loves to talk. People were beginning to say that you were either kidnapped by the Romans because of your beauty, or a wild animal had killed you. Because of that, Amos the wine dresser began pushing for me to take one of his daughters to marry. He was very insistent and persistent. There is a reason he is very successful; he doesn't take no for an answer!" Joseph shook his head. "I told him I wouldn't consider another bride until I knew what had happened to you."

"Are people talking about me?" Miriam asked.

"Uhhh … yes. They don't know about the baby so much, but your disappearance has everyone talking," Joseph said. "But don't let any of that bother you."

Miriam followed Joseph's gaze to her small baby bump. "It's impossible," she smiled, "but it is happening."

Joseph nodded. He reached his hand out towards her. "Can I?"

Miriam nodded.

He gently touched her tummy. "Nothing is impossible with God," he smiled back at her.

"Miriam, Joseph, come inside for some food," Elizabeth called from the back door. Joseph helped Miriam up, and he took her hand in his as they walked into the house. Miriam could feel herself melt inside.

Zachariah and Elizabeth welcomed them around the table where they enjoyed a delicious meal of chicken and chickpea stew with fresh bread on the side. As they sat around the table, Elizabeth and Zachariah shared the story about baby John. And as Zachariah does best, he made everyone laugh through the whole story.

"So now that you are back together by the divine will of God," said Elizabeth, "what do you intend to do?" She changed the subject as she passed a plate full of fresh juicy orange slices to Joseph.

"That's a good question," Joseph said as he took a slice of orange. "I wish to bring Miriam back home to Nazareth, where I am running a carpentry shop. I am doing very well there. Though I hesitate, due to the gossip of our dear neighbors, since Miriam is the talk of the town right now. But I did promise to bring her home to her family."

"You're not from the Galilee," Zachariah stated. "You don't have the Galilean accent."

"True," said Joseph. "I was born in Bethlehem. For various reasons I don't wish to talk about it. I decided to move in with my uncle who lives in Nazareth to work with him in carpentry."

"What about having your wedding here?" Zachariah proposed. "And then you can either return to Bethlehem, or you could stay here as long as you want – well, as long as you mind your keep, of course."

"I would never go back to Bethlehem. And thank you for your kind and generous offer." Joseph turned to Miriam and smiled at her. "I suppose I should talk to Miriam about all of this."

Miriam blushed. She felt all giddy inside!

Zachariah pulled out his sitar and Miriam and Elizabeth got up and started to dance together around the room.

That night as Miriam laid in her bed, her mind wouldn't dare rest. She went over and over the whole scenario in the back garden. From a very terrifying moment to the most joyous thing that could ever be thought possible had happened! A door she thought was shut forever, had suddenly swung wide open. Her crushed dreams had now come back to life.

"Miriam?"

Miriam's thoughts were interrupted by a soft knock on her door. She wrapped a blanket around herself and opened up the door just a crack.

Joseph stood there with a lamp in his hand. "I'm sorry to bother you, but the stars are stunning to look at tonight, and I was wondering if you could join me for a little bit?" he asked with a big smile. *Irresistible!*

"Of course!" Miriam slipped out the back door of the house with Joseph. He took her hand. She looked up into the night sky. Joseph was right. Up above them was a beautiful display of starry hosts! She glanced at him as he was looking up.

Noticing her gaze, he looked down at her lovingly. "Will you come home with me?" he asked. "Your house is ready in Nazareth."

"With all my heart!" she exclaimed. "I will follow you to the ends of the earth!" She embraced Joseph. "God is good!"

"I don't know what the future holds for us," said Joseph, "for all *three* of us in Nazareth, but we have each other. We will have a small wedding celebration. I already told your father that if I found you, I would bring you home to be my wife."

"I think the baby bump is still small enough to hide," said Miriam, patting her tummy.

7 THE RING & THE DOXOLOGY

Zachariah and Elizabeth blessed the lovebirds on their decision to return to Nazareth. Joseph loaded the wagon with food and supplies that they would need for the journey home.

Miriam stood next to the wagon just in awe of everything that had transpired. She felt very happy and giddy inside. She was going home and was excited about her wedding that she had longed for. It probably wasn't going to be quite the wedding she had first hoped for, but even if it was just with her family and some close friends, she would be overjoyed!

"Thank you, Elizabeth and Zachariah, for taking me in so graciously. I will cherish this time that we had together," Miriam said as she embraced them and gave John a kiss on the head. "And I will miss this sweet, sweet boy!"

Joseph then helped Miriam onto the wagon, and soon they were off. Miriam waved goodbye as the wagon lurched forward and they began their journey back to Nazareth.

It would be a long four to five-day journey by wagon and donkey. They travelled by day, and in the evenings, they joined other travelers as they camped out under the stars. Miriam enjoyed the end of the day when they would sit around the fire with the other travelers swapping stories, sharing meals and playing music together.

For sleeping at night, Joseph let Miriam sleep in the wagon, and he slept outside by the campfire with some of the other travelers.

On the last day of their travels, Miriam finally had the courage to ask Joseph some of the questions that were troubling her. "Joseph, how is my father?" Miriam asked. For most of the journey, they had talked about their new house, Joseph's carpentry business, how many children they were going to have together, her wedding dress that she had almost finished before she had run away and subjects that were easy to talk about.

"Well, to be honest," sighed Joseph, "it's been difficult. Your father is an extraordinary man, very well-respected in the town. Naturally, your disappearance troubled him greatly." Joseph glanced at Miriam. She had always wished to be in his favor and be the daughter that would delight his heart. Her being mysteriously pregnant had turned her whole world upside down.

"Did you tell him your dream?" Miriam asked.

"I did. He was astonished. He had no words. Your father is a righteous man and wants to do things according to the law of our people. So he wants to only do the right thing." Joseph paused. "We are in a situation which no human has ever traversed. People want to say this is wrong or that is right. But when something is miraculous, or when we don't understand what is happening, it takes a little bit of faith and patience to figure things out. So we talked about it. He is willing to give his blessing for us to have a wedding and for you to come into my home and be my wife." Joseph smiled.

"So the town is talking about me? What do they say?" Miriam asked.

"Everyone is wondering what happened to you. Rumors are flying about why a sweet, happy young lady that comes from a loving family would disappear without a trace. Some think you may have been attacked, or a Roman fell in love with you and took you away … So there are many stories flying around. Everyone is offering me their opinion and advice. They think they are being very helpful, which is kind of them, of course, but after a while, it is very exhausting. No one knows that you are pregnant though, only your family and I," Joseph said. "I think I would prefer for people to find out that you are pregnant *after* our wedding … So if you wouldn't mind keeping it a secret for now." Joseph looked at Miriam.

"That's kind of hard when I am growing a bump here," she protested a little.

"I'm sure you can hide it. You're not that big yet!"

"We can try," Miriam agreed with a sigh. She was tired of hiding things.

"Don't be afraid," said Joseph. "Miriam, the town will soon forget. Let us do our best to live a normal God-fearing life and allow God to do what He wills." He smiled and roughed up her hair a little.

Miriam smiled and playfully pushed his hand away.

They stopped at a well to water the donkey. Joseph helped Miriam down from the wagon. She filled her jug with water and then lifted it to her lips to drink. It was refreshing and invigorating on a hot day.

There was a small hut where a man was selling some fresh produce to the travelers passing by.

"Hello, my dear!" the merchant exclaimed. "Would you like some apples for your journey? I also have here some red peppers and melon! Oh, I know you will love the melon!"

"Thank you, but I must be on my way," Miriam tried to excuse herself gracefully.

He suddenly took his knife and sliced through the red flesh of the melon and handed her a slice. "No need to thank me," the man smiled. "Just enjoy, my dear daughter!"

Miriam smiled and took the slice of melon. Joseph came to Miriam's side. "We will take the whole melon, actually," Joseph said. He pulled a coin out of his pouch and handed it to the man.

"I dare say I never!" The man took Joseph's hand and was fixated upon the gold ring on his finger. Joseph quickly pulled his hand away.

"How did that ever become your property? It has the symbol of King Solomon!"

"I think we better be going. Thank you for the melon." Joseph dragged Miriam away with him back to the wagon while balancing the melon in his other hand. But the man wouldn't leave him alone and followed them to the wagon.

"Either you are a thief, or you inherited such a gift!" the man persisted. "That is something that couldn't possibly be bought, could it?"

"No, it is not for sale, and I am not a thief," Joseph said firmly. He turned to help Miriam onto the wagon. She was a bit curious about why Joseph was trying to avoid the inquiries from the man. She had noticed the ring on Joseph's finger before, and when she asked about it, he had said that his father had given it to him. She didn't understand why this man was so obsessed by the ring.

"God bless you, son of David! May there one day be a Son of David upon the throne again!"

the man shouted as Joseph also climbed onto the wagon bench and then signaled for the donkey to resume their journey.

Miriam looked at Joseph with curiosity. He seemed annoyed with the man who had been overcome with curiosity about his ring. She put her hand in his hand. He didn't flinch; his eyes were lost in a gaze of days gone by. Miriam waited until her ability to be patient had been maxed out.

"Joseph?" she asked.

No answer.

"Hello Joseph, where are you?" she asked with a little tease.

He didn't even blink.

She nudged him slightly, and then suddenly he returned. He shook his head. "I am sorry!" Joseph laughed at himself.

"What happened here and what happened there with that man?" Miriam asked. Joseph sighed.

"This ring dates very far back in my family," Joseph said slowly. He looked down at it on his finger. "It was King Solomon's signet ring. I don't like to tell people, so as not to draw too much attention to myself. So I would appreciate it if you would help keep my secret." He raised an eyebrow at her hoping for her agreement.

"Your secret is safe with me... but...." Miriam continued to pry. "What do you mean it was King Solomon's signet ring? Do you mean THE King Solomon? The King who built the first Temple? Son of David? Wisest King of Israel?"

"Precisely. Nice to hear that you listen to what the Rabbis ramble on about in the synagogue," Joseph smirked sarcastically.

"How did you get it?"

"The ring was passed down to the firstborn of every son down the line of King Solomon. Even after the Kingdom of Judah was destroyed by Babylon, the tradition continued, even though since the destruction of Judah and our exile into Babylon, we are no longer kings."

"They passed it down to *you?* That would mean ... you would have been the King of Judah if the dynasty had been maintained after the Babylonian exile?" Miriam asked with astonishment and excitement.

Joseph looked uncomfortable. "You come up with quick conclusions, my dear. If the firstborn of every son continued to sit on the throne of David, then, most likely, yes." Joseph nodded his head.

"That's unbelievable!" Miriam exclaimed.

"It is what it is," Joseph muttered.

"My family also comes from the line of David, but not through King Solomon, but through his other son, Nathan," Miriam said. "And it was prophesied that the Messiah would be a Son of David!" She excitedly put the pieces together in her head.

"Now I know you spend too much time in the synagogue!" Joseph laughed at Miriam's knowledge of the Torah.

"My father loves telling stories of the Bible, and often talks about the Messiah and who He might be. I felt that it was so random that I would be chosen to be the mother of the Messiah. But maybe it's not, maybe it's Destiny!" She threw her arms in the air.

"Perhaps. However, I believe we are all just people, doesn't matter who you are or where you come from. We all need to earn our keep in this world, and live a life according to God's Commandments. That's it. I'm hoping to live a quiet life, to raise a family together and enjoy this time we have on earth. I don't believe in chasing fantasies or prestige. And I think that even as parents of the 'Messiah', we should raise him like we would any other child. To be a hard worker, to earn his keep and to fear the Lord. And God will lead him into whatever destiny he has. And, Lord willing, when the time is right, He will restore the Kingdom of Israel and lead our people in following the Lord," Joseph said firmly.

Miriam nodded thoughtfully. "Very well, king of my heart," she said, giving him a sweet smile.

Soon, the little town of Nazareth was in view. Miriam suddenly felt nervous. She tried to imagine how they might react when they saw her. The fear of death was taken away since Joseph had miraculously stepped in to redeem her from all shame.

As they started to pull into the town, neighbors came outside of their homes to witness their return. They waved, some shouted greetings and blessings, while others whispered to each other and pointed.

Joseph turned the wagon towards Miriam's family's home. She could see it in the distance. Her whole family was waiting outside the house. Miriam felt like her stomach was in knots and her heart began to beat harder and harder as they got closer and closer.

When at last they reached the house, Miriam's father quickly came to the side of the wagon where Miriam sat and put his arms out to help her down from the wagon. And without missing a beat, she was soon buried within a warm grizzly hug. She could feel the rest of her family also surround and embrace them. Her eyes filled with tears as she realized the pain they had gone through. As the hugs were released, she dropped to the ground and bowed down.

"I am terribly sorry for the pain and worry I have caused you all," Miriam apologized. "I sought refuge with our cousin Elizabeth and Zachariah who just welcomed their own newborn baby into their lives."

"Miriam, Miriam, my daughter," her father exclaimed, "you have caused me more grey hairs than the whole rest of the children combined!"

"I'm sorry, Abba."

"What do you mean Elizabeth had a baby?" Miriam's mother asked. "She is beyond child-bearing age, is she not?"

"It's another miracle!" said Miriam. "The angel told me that Elizabeth had conceived in her old age. And I had to see if it was true, and it was!"

They looked at Joseph to see if he had also been witness to this miracle.

"It's true," said Joseph. "They named him John."

"We need to talk," Miriam's father said. "Please come inside and let us have a moment to discuss the matter at hand in the privacy of our home."

"First, we will let the travelers wash up a little," said Miriam's mother. She handed Joseph a jug of water and Miriam a towel. They washed their faces, hands, and feet and then entered the home.

They sat around the table. Miriam's sister, Hannah, handed them goblets of water to drink and some dried fruits and nuts to nourish them.

Miriam's father sat at the end of the table; he began pulling on his beard. Miriam was worried that he would actually tug a few hairs out.

"Dear family, we welcome home our dear daughter, Miriam. Miriam, it is good that you came back. You have worried us beyond reason. And not to imagine our fears for your condition. So now we are, at present, all back together. Bless the Lord! My daughter here is pregnant, which is known only to us. She claims that an angel came and told her that she would conceive supernaturally.

"At first, I thought it was pure blasphemy. I was suspicious of foul play. I felt inclined to let Joseph know. To no one's surprise, he was also very upset that his betrothed was pregnant, and he was also suspicious of foul play. After this was all discovered, and our emotions were hitting the roof, we all went to bed, with the decision that I would go and bring this matter before the Rabbinical council in our town. Joseph said that he decided that night that he would most likely divorce her quietly so as not to make a public display of the matter.

So, in the morning, before I went to the elders, I discovered that my daughter had disappeared without a trace. And then Joseph came to the house. To my astonishment, he said that God had spoken to him in a dream and told him that Miriam had indeed conceived supernaturally, and no ordinary child, but the Messiah, by the Holy Spirit.

"So, what do I do? I am just a man! A humble man. Never has an angel given me a message or has God spoken to me in a dream. And then, angels begin giving messages to my children under my roof! My roof! And how am I, just a man, to handle this situation and bring some order here? Now, Joseph has agreed to marry my pregnant daughter who supposedly never slept with a man! This is crazy!

"So while Joseph was away to see if he could find Miriam in Jerusalem, I went to the elders. I didn't tell them that Miriam was pregnant. I just asked them one single question. I asked… 'So… how will we know who the Messiah is? Are there any signs?' Yaron the head Rabbi said the most amazing thing." He paused. His eyes grew big, and they welled up with tears.

"He said that the prophet Isaiah prophesied that God would provide a sign, that lo, a *virgin* will conceive and bring forth a son and his name will be Immanuel!" His voice broke as he tried to maintain his composure.

"When I heard this, I was shattered inside. As a simple, God-fearing Jewish man, I am wrecked! Miriam – in your womb is the promised seed of Abraham, the Son of David! He is coming! Our salvation draws nigh!" he declared as his voice cracked with emotion. He stood up and placed his hands on Miriam and Joseph.

"I bless you both, as God has chosen you both to help usher in the Messianic Age." He bent down and gave them both a big wet kiss on the cheek.

There was not a dry eye in the room.

8 UNEXPECTED

Miriam and her family went into marriage preparation right away. With the help of her sister and mother, they pulled out her beautiful ornate wedding dress and gave it a few final finishing touches it needed for it to be ready. They did their best to make sure that it would safely disguise Miriam's pregnancy. There was also endless cooking and baking that went on in the kitchen from sunrise to sunset. It was a flurry of nonstop activity as the family prepared for a feast that would essentially be enough to feed the whole village if need be. Her brothers and her father headed over to Joseph's home, where he prepared the courtyard as an area for hosting their guests and built a chuppah (canopy) where the marriage ceremony would take place.

For Miriam it was all very exhausting – but exciting at the same time.

Then, the night that Miriam thought would never come ... arrived! As the sun was setting, there was a loud shofar blast that echoed throughout the whole village, announcing the coming bride groom who was on his way to meet his bride. Miriam was dressed in her beautiful wedding dress with the blue scarf that Rachel gave her to conceal her five-month pregnant belly. Her father came into the room upstairs and clasped a gold necklace around her neck and handed her bracelets and earrings to wear. Her mother pulled the veil over her face, then her father and mother linked arms with Miriam, and led her out of the house to where family, friends, and the villagers awaited with excitement. Everyone cheered when they walked through the gate of the family's courtyard. Miriam's parents continued to lead her through the crowd to Joseph's house.

    A whole procession followed, playing music on harps and rejoicing with tambourines. Miriam's sister and her girlfriends had small oil lamps to lead the way to Joseph's home. Miriam looked at her parents with gratefulness as they ushered her towards her groom. As they neared Joseph's house, she kept feeling her emotions rise within her. Tears came to her eyes as she saw dimly through the veil her handsome Joseph standing at the gate with a huge smile on his face. What a miracle it was!

    "Welcome, my bride!" Joseph greeted her as they got close. Miriam's father put his hands on Joseph's head and blessed him. Then he did the same to Miriam. Miriam then gave each parent a loving embrace, then turned to Joseph, who held out his arm to her. She happily linked arms with Joseph, and he led her through the gates of their new home! Together they walked under the chuppah where the Rabbi stood waiting for them.

Joseph then turned to Miriam and lifted the veil off her face. She smiled excitedly at Joseph and at the same time happy tears spilled down her cheeks. Then the Rabbi recited several blessings and sang songs over the new couple. He handed Joseph a goblet of wine and blessed it. Joseph took a sip, then handed it to Miriam. She sipped the wine. The Rabbi said some more blessings, then they took the empty wine cup and placed it on the ground. Joseph then smashed it under his sandaled foot. The broken cup was a traditional symbol to never forget Jerusalem as their chief joy. The crowd erupted with songs of joy! The moment was electric with excitement and soon the musicians were blasting their horns and strumming their harps and stringed instruments, and everyone began celebrating in dance! Miriam began dancing with the girls while Joseph danced with the men. Then there was food and the wine. Everyone feasted and danced late into the night.

As the last guests departed and her family kissed her good night and goodbye, Miriam and Joseph entered their new home to spend their first night together as a married couple.

Miriam's heart fluttered a little.

Joseph bent down and kissed his beautiful bride. Then he helped her remove the jewelry and unbraid her hair. He sighed.

Miriam looked up with wonder. "What's wrong, Joseph?" she asked.

"This is a holy moment for us, but I believe that what is inside of you is even more holy. I can hardly believe I am saying this … but we should wait until after the baby is born to consummate our marriage." Joseph shook his head with disbelief at himself for being so bold.

"You think?" Miriam asked.

"The prophecy from Isaiah that your father told us about keeps running through my mind: 'the *virgin* will conceive and bring forth a son,'" Joseph said. "If we make love tonight, will you still be a virgin?" Joseph asked. "I've learnt the hard way to not go against your conscience … and I for one would not want to get in the way of what God is doing here and with you. So, we will need to be patient, my love." Joseph stroked her long dark hair.

Miriam sighed. "Patient indeed!" She smiled.

"No sweet smiles, Miriam, or you will make this very hard on us!" Joseph teased her. Then he pulled her close and kissed her passionately.

The next couple of months passed by quickly. Miriam was nearing the end of her pregnancy. There was no hiding it now from the villagers' curious eyes. As Joseph had requested, Miriam spoke to no one about the angel, or that she was carrying inside her the Messiah of Israel. People made comments that they were surprised at how quickly she had become pregnant, or how big she had gotten so quickly. Miriam would just smile and quickly change the subject from how far along she was in her pregnancy to advice on how to care for a new baby. This always worked well, since almost everyone had a strong opinion on how best to take care of a baby.

One day, Miriam was in the market to purchase some dye for some of the baby clothes she had woven and sewed together.

"Miriam!"

Miriam turned around to see her old childhood friend Beulah. Beulah had fiery red curly hair, fair skin and freckles. She smiled and greeted her with a kiss on each cheek.

"How are you, Beulah?" Miriam asked.

Beulah had three little children holding on to the skirts of her robe.

"Blessed be the Lord, we are all well and healthy. But you will soon see, having children is literally what the good proverb says, *your lamp does not go out at night, and it's not out of choice!*" she half-laughed and half-groaned. Miriam chuckled as she patted one of her little daughters on the head.

"It's been so long since we've spent time together. Why don't you come by my place for tea?" Miriam asked.

"I would love that. I do miss you, Miriam! But you know how it is, life with my three little ones has me scurrying from morning to night! But my dear, it is you I want to hear about! Is it true that you ran away to Jerusalem by yourself?" Beulah inquired. "I hear little whispers here and there. I would love to know what really happened."

Suddenly Beulah's husband walked over. He looked down at Miriam suspiciously. He was one of the teachers in the synagogue and was known for being very strict and uncompromising in keeping the Torah.

"Beulah, take the children and start making your way home." he said in a deep, authoritative voice.

Beulah nodded her head submissively and led her children in the direction of their home.

Miriam suddenly became very nervous. She had known Beulah and her husband Rabbi Boaz all her life, but since Beulah's early marriage and since she had become a mother, Miriam saw less and less of her. Miriam always felt a little afraid of Rabbi Boaz, perhaps because he was quite a bit older than her and Beulah, or maybe it was because he always seemed a bit cold. But nonetheless, she had a great respect for him as a great teacher.

"I want you to stay away from my wife," he said very sternly.

Miriam flushed. Several protests came to her mind, but somehow she managed to hold her tongue from shooting back.

"I am watching you and am concerned about your purity. I'm not sure if Joseph is aware of any such possibilities, but as a father I have noticed that you have become quite pregnant very fast." He spoke slowly, which felt like torture to Miriam's ears.

"I will respect your wishes," Miriam mumbled with a slight bow, then turned to leave.

A big crowd had begun to gather in the marketplace and she could hear someone shouting out some announcement. Miriam was too shook up to stay and listen, rather she pushed her way through the crowd as fast as she could to get as far away from Rabbi Boaz as possible. The encounter with him made her feel very uncomfortable.

When she got back to the house, Miriam buried herself in housework and preparing the evening meal, which helped her forget Rabbi Boaz.

Soon Joseph came home from working in the shop. "Miriam, I'm home!" He held in his arms a large item covered in a cloth. He had a big smile on his face.

Miriam looked up from the table where she was chopping up some vegetables. Her eyes lit up. "What is it?" she asked.

Joseph put it down and lifted up the cloth. It was a beautiful little cradle with little animals carved into it.

"Oh, Joseph, it's beautiful!" Miriam exclaimed.

"And look! Best of all …" He rocked the cradle back and forth.

"That's amazing! I've never seen anything like it!" Miriam wiped her hands on a cloth and then came over to Joseph's side and rocked it herself.

"It's the most amazing cradle!" Miriam smiled. "Perfect for our baby Messiah!"

Joseph kissed his wife. "It smells amazing in here! I see you are involved in more miracles than one!" Joseph laughed.

Miriam put the food on the table. There was a loaf of fresh bread and some balsamic and olive oil to dip it in; then there were sliced vegetables and a spicy lentil stew. Together, they sat by the table with Joseph's arm around Miriam. They talked about their day and laughed together. She refrained from telling Joseph about what Rabbi Boaz had said, so as not to cause him to worry. Her life with Joseph seemed perfect at the moment; she couldn't be happier or more content. With him she felt safe and secure.

Suddenly, there was a knock on the door. Miriam and Joseph looked at each other in surprise. Then the door opened up; it was her brother Simon.

"Simon, come in!" Joseph waved his arm for Simon to sit down.

"Thank you, sorry to disturb you," he said. He sat down and eagerly ripped off a piece of the fresh bread and dipped it in the balsamic vinegar and took a bite.

"You would think that you've never been fed!" Miriam teased. Simon smirked at her.

"I have something very serious to say," Simon said as he swallowed his food.

"Such as?" Joseph raised his eyebrows.

"I was in the market, and there was an important announcement. A Roman centurion announced to everyone an edict from the Roman leader. It says that there is a census and every man needs to register in their town of birth."

"Are you serious?" Joseph asked with disgust.

"You can read the edict, it is posted in the town center in the market," Simon said. "Most of the people in our town are born here. I think you and a few others are the only ones who will need to travel for this," Simon said, filling a bowl of stew for himself.

"This means I will need to travel to Bethlehem!" Joseph sighed. "Do you know when this needs to be done by?"

"Before the Feast of Tabernacles."

"Between now and then Miriam could have the baby!" Joseph exclaimed with frustration. "It will take me at least 10 days to go to Bethlehem and back, and with all the travelers in town for the Feast of Tabernacles and for the edict it will slow me down."

"Joseph, I want you to be with me when the baby comes," Miriam protested.

"I'll be back before the baby is born." Joseph tried to calm her fears. "You can stay with your family and I'll be home before you know it," he assured her.

"Women in my family usually carry our babies longer than most women, so I hope it is as you say," Miriam sighed, patting her belly nervously.

That night as they lay in bed, Miriam tossed and turned. She couldn't stop thinking of Joseph leaving and Rabbi Boaz's words.

Her movements woke Joseph up and he put his hand on her shoulder. "Miriam, it is going to be okay," he whispered in the darkness of the night.

"I'm afraid, Joseph," Miriam whispered back.

"About what?"

"Of what people will say or do when the baby is born." Miriam said. She then could no longer hold back about her encounter with Rabbi Boaz.

"What if he accuses me of adultery or something?" Miriam worried.

"I can't believe he said that to you!" Joseph fumed. "How dare he, I will speak to him at once about this!"

"No, Joseph, please don't! I think it will make matters only worse. He will then demand an answer of why I am pregnant before we were married." Miriam said. She thought for a moment. "Or what if we just tell people the truth that I am having the Messiah?"

"Do you think they will believe you?" Joseph asked. "And if they believe, just imagine the pressure and expectations our baby will have from people as he grows up here?"

"It would just make things easier for us, no?" Miriam pondered.

"I have my doubts, my dear." Joseph shook his head. "I see we are not quite out of danger." He sighed.

They were silent for a moment.

"Joseph ... I will come with you to Bethlehem," Miriam said decidedly.

"What?" Joseph sat up in bed. "This journey is no place for someone who is about to give birth!"

"We can take it very slow," Miriam suggested. "Maybe I can have the baby in one of the villages on the way to Bethlehem. We will be amongst people who don't know our situation. Then we can return once we have passed nine months since our marriage. So people will never know the circumstances. The baby will be a couple months old already, but maybe it will be okay?"

"It's not a very good idea ... but ... we may not have a choice. Do you think you would be up for the journey?" Joseph asked.

"I am strong and healthy." Miriam took Joseph's hand and gave it a squeeze.

The next day Joseph and Miriam began preparations for their journey to Bethlehem. When they explained the plan to Miriam's family, they at first protested, but soon came around to their reasoning, especially when Miriam told them about the confrontation with Rabbi Boaz.

9 THE PAST

It was now mid-September, getting close to the Feast of Tabernacles. The roads were crowded with people traveling to their town of birth for the census and for the upcoming holiday. Many Jewish people who lived abroad and many of those living within, often would travel to Jerusalem for the Feast of Tabernacles. Miriam and Joseph set out with their covered wagon and donkey very early in the morning to avoid the heat of the day. They tried to make sure the journey would be as comfortable as possible for Miriam, with pillows and blankets in the back of the wagon for her to recline on.

When they had reached about midday, they stopped along the road to find refuge from the hot sun. They stopped in the shade of the trees. Joseph watered the donkey as Miriam unpacked some food for Joseph and herself for their noon day meal.

"I think after a nice rest, we will be able to make it to Beit Shean before sundown," Joseph predicted. "I have a cousin that lives there. Hopefully we will be able to stay with him."

"That would be a blessing!" Miriam fanned herself profusely with a wicker fan.

"Miriam, why not cool yourself by wading in the spring?" Joseph suggested. He tied up the donkey and then helped Miriam to the fresh cool spring hidden behind the trees. They removed their tunics, leaving only their robes on. Miriam lifted up the skirt of her robe and waded in the refreshing waters, with Joseph holding her arm so she wouldn't fall.

"This is amazing!" Miriam exclaimed.

"A little bit of paradise!" Joseph agreed. He bent down and washed his face, then he looked up at Miriam and playfully splashed her with the water.

"Oh no, you don't!" Miriam gasped and then returned the favor by splashing him back. Soon they were both drenched, but now fully cooled down from the hot sun.

"Oh dear, look at us!" Miriam laughed as she wrung the water from her long hair. They then sat on a blanket under a tree and ate their noon meal and fell asleep.

When they woke up, they continued on their journey to Beit Shean, and just like Joseph predicted, they arrived before the sun went down. Beit Shean was one of cities of the Decapolis. Under the Roman occupation, it was heavily influenced by the Roman culture. The city was very elaborate with a large amphitheater, marble pillars imported from Rome and bath houses for the soldiers in the city center.

They entered through one of the gates. Joseph asked the tax collector sitting by the gate the whereabouts of his cousin.

"You go right, then make a left, and then a right, and then another right, and there you will find his house." The tax collector waved his arms in all directions.

"I will need more specific directions than that." Joseph tried again. The tax collector turned to a little boy standing by him.

"Boy, lead this couple to Reuven the goldsmith," he ordered the young boy. The young boy, about twelve years old, nodded his head, took hold of the harness of the donkey and helped lead Miriam and Joseph through the cobbled streets of Beit Shean.

"Here we are," the boy announced when they reached the gate of a prominent-looking house.

Joseph jumped down from the wagon and handed the boy a coin. "Thank you, my son."

The boy smiled and ran off.

Joseph knocked loudly on the gate.

Soon the gate opened. A young man who looked no older than sixteen years old stepped outside the courtyard. A big smile spread across his face when he saw Joseph.

"Joseph!" he exclaimed, and gave him a big hug.

"Avner, my boy! You have grown so much since I saw you last!" Joseph patted him on the shoulder.

Avner helped Joseph and Miriam put their donkey in the barn and the wagon in the courtyard. Then he led them into the beautiful home of Joseph's cousin, Reuven the goldsmith. They were warmly welcomed and given a hearty meal of beef stew and vegetables.

"Really, Joseph, you should have come to Beit Shean with me instead of Nazareth! Business is great here! Being a carpenter in a small tiny village, you must be bored out of your mind!" Reuven bellowed as he sloshed some wine down. "But of course, you found a very beautiful wife, congratulations!" he said noticing the look on Miriam's face.

"I do not regret my decision one bit. I enjoy the quiet life in the hills of the Galilee. It's now home for me." Joseph said contently. He looked at Miriam and smiled.

"But look at how fine of a life you can have here, and not to mention the business potential!" Reuven persisted.

"I've had my share of the 'fine life', complete with the constant banter of politics," Joseph said firmly. "In Nazareth, I can go about my business without anyone pressuring me about politics or pushing me around because of their great ideas for me."

"What a waste!" Reuven scoffed. "You would have made a great leader! If only you would have tried a little harder."

Miriam sat quietly, confused about what exactly they were talking about. She realized then that she didn't know very much about Joseph's life before Nazareth.

"That is enough!" Joseph slammed his fist on the table, causing everyone in the room to jump. Miriam looked at Joseph in surprise.

"Never mind." Reuven finally changed the subject and began to talk about himself and his goldsmith business. Then he talked about his previous marriage to his deceased wife and his new marriage to his new wife, and what it was like to raise two families together.

Some time later, the weary travelers were finally released to the guest room chambers, where they soon fell fast asleep.

The next morning Reuven showed off some of his craftsmanship and went on talking throughout the breakfast meal about how fine and wonderful Beit Shean was and how Joseph and Miriam should move there.

Afterwards, when the two of them were in the hallway, Joseph whispered to her, "How do you feel, Miriam?"

"I feel okay ... maybe a little tired, but I would like to get on the road again."

"Good," said Joseph. "I am ready to go from here myself. This city feels a little too cramped and a little too 'Roman' for me."

Miriam nodded her head in agreement.

Later that hot, dusty day, after a couple hours of traveling down the road that trailed along the Jordan River in the Jordan Valley, Miriam was beginning to feel tired of lying down or sitting. She could not manage to find a comfortable position in the back of the wagon. "Joseph," she said, wiping her damp brow, "do you think we could stop for a moment and I could walk around a bit?"

Joseph agreed and pulled over. He gently helped her down from the wagon.

She stretched and moved around to get the uncomfortable kinks in her body to loosen up.

"I'm so sorry, my dear, that you have to go through this." Joseph handed Miriam a jug of water to drink from.

"It's okay," she smiled. "It's just that I am not accustomed to being stationary. But you know, I am looking forward to meeting your family in Bethlehem. You don't talk about them much." Miriam looked at Joseph curiously.

Joseph took a deep breath and ran his fingers through his dark curly hair.

"What is it?" Miriam asked.

"It's hard for me," Joseph muttered.

"Hard because of what?" Miriam prodded.

"As you know, my father passed away, leaving my mother a widow, a year after my bar mitzvah. When he died, all expectations of a leader fell on me as the oldest child in the family. My father had been a figurehead leader for the people in Bethlehem, very respected and loved. He held a kind of diplomatic leadership position between the people in Bethlehem and King Herod and his palace. And so I guess people assumed that I would naturally take his place. People even went further to hope that I would be a leader for our people because of my family tree. I felt so much pressure to be someone special and be like … like a … Messiah, I suppose. They wanted me to be the next Matisyahu Maccabee, the hero who led the defeat against the Greeks!" Joseph laughed.

His face clouded over. "Then, something dreadful happened which caused me to abandon everything and leave Bethlehem. I left a coward, really, and I am ashamed to go back and show my face there." Joseph sighed.

Miriam frowned.

"I'm sorry that I am only telling you this now, Miriam … Your respect and admiration for me as just a carpenter is all I want in this world." He looked at her pleadingly.

"Of course, Joseph," Miriam said, trying to reassure him. "I love and respect you."

"So you now know about my family line," Joseph continued. "My family was and is very prominent in Bethlehem, amongst the Sadducees. We could have whatever we wanted, whenever we wanted. We were friends with King Herod and his family and we were invited to all of the royal banquets.

"It was several years after my father had passed away, when this man named Ezra kept coming to our home and telling us story after story about our nation and how we need to stand up for our people and not be enslaved by Rome.

"My younger brother Seth became especially zealous about what Ezra was talking about and began participating in some of his rebel plans to turn against the Roman Empire. He also began training to fight. And slowly, I also became involved, mostly motivated by peer pressure that my younger brother might appear more of a leader than me. So Ezra had us use our relationship with Herod's palace, in order to obtain secrets and information to pass on to him.

"It became a game of adrenaline, and the attention and admiration we received from others went to our heads. Everyone looked up to Seth and me, and people kept saying that we were going to be the saviors of Israel, which was flattering and definitely boosted our already fat egos!" Joseph shook his head.

"Then, the worst thing happened …" Joseph sighed.

Miriam took his hand.

"Ezra had sent me on a mission to obtain information about a caravan from Rome that was supposed to arrive in Jerusalem. I had no idea what Ezra was up to and what he had planned for this caravan. So I went to the palace and with charm and ease snuck into the general's quarters and stole the scroll with the information and delivered it to Ezra. A couple of days later, Ezra came to our house late at night and handed Seth and me swords and daggers. Ezra said no one was going to get hurt, but that the weapons were to be used only to intimidate the coming caravan.

At first, I refused, because something inside didn't feel right about the situation, but Seth immediately agreed. Ezra then said that Seth was an example to all of the people, a true warrior and an upcoming leader of Israel. So ... not to look like a coward, I went with them.

"This caravan held Elisha Ben Uri, a prominent and influential scholar from Hebron. He had been imprisoned for saying that the Roman Empire was barbaric, and for protesting publicly at the pagan activities that were being practiced by the Romans. The plan was to rescue him from the Roman soldiers who were bringing him to Jerusalem where he was going to be most likely sentenced to death for blaspheming against the Roman Empire.

"So that night we went with Ezra. We came upon the caravan as planned, and Ezra, who was on horseback, stood in front of the caravan to block their passage. He then demanded the release of Elisha Ben Uri. There were about five Roman soldiers there, and they refused to do what Ezra demanded, and so Ezra pulled out his sword. The plan was for Ezra to distract the soldiers while Seth and I would secretly release the prisoner from inside the wagon. So, as Ezra knew how to do best, he talked in a persuasive manner which had the men locked on him.

"As he talked and waved his sword around to intimidate the soldiers, we snuck behind the wagon and lifted the bar that held the prison door shut. Elisha Ben Uri was shocked to see us, but quietly followed us out of the wagon and towards the woods. We were almost there when one of the Roman soldiers saw us and began chasing us. We then began running for our lives!

"They recaptured Elisha Ben Uri. But worst of all, they started to shoot arrows and my brother Seth was struck in the stomach. I somehow picked him up and was able to bring him home undetected. But when I reached our house, he had lost too much blood, and the next morning … he passed away." Joseph shook his head sadly.

"I'm sorry to hear this." Miriam wrapped her arms around her husband. "Did Ezra survive?"

"He did. And tried to convince me that my brother had died a worthy death But in my eyes, he was responsible for my brother's death. People kept asking me if I would seek revenge, and they would say all kinds of crazy things. I decided I just needed to leave, and that was what led me to Nazareth to be a carpenter in my uncle's shop. I am not a man of the sword; I love the beauty and quiet of the Galilee where you and I can raise a family together. I have felt so much freedom and that I can just be myself there, and I don't need to wear any disguise." Joseph shrugged his shoulders.

"Joseph, you never told me anything about this, about you being like a spy and joining the rebels!" Miriam exclaimed. "It's very dangerous!"

"I allowed myself to be pressured into it. I admit it was exciting at first, and I believed I was doing it for our nation, but I am not the hero that people hoped I would be. Nor the leader. I probably wouldn't make a good king, if things had turned out that way. I'm just a humble carpenter, and I am happy being that."

"Tsk, Joseph ..." Miriam clicked her tongue. "I don't even know where to begin! First, I'm shocked that you kept this information from me and second I'm so sorry to hear about your brother Seth ... and thirdly ... I ... I don't know what to say. I mean ... you are ... my hero and I don't think you need to feel that you need to meet anyone's expectations. I believe you and I ... together... we are fulfilling our God-given purpose of life, which is probably far bigger than what we even know."

Joseph pulled Miriam close to him and kissed her gently. "Please God," he sighed.

Joseph then helped Miriam back onto the wagon where she lay down in the back, and then he jumped onto the bench. He took the thick leather reins in his hands and snapped them against the donkey's back. The donkey lurched forward slowly, and they continued on their journey. Miriam slowly drifted to sleep.

10 IMMANUEL

Miriam awoke, feeling very uncomfortable lying down in the back of the wagon. She could feel her belly contract gently, but it wasn't strong enough to take her breath away. She tried to ignore the feeling, hoping it would go away. She turned over into another position to see if that would help, but contractions continued to come consistently. The worrisome thought entered her mind that she might be possibly going into labor, but she quickly tried to dispel the thought.

It had been a slow week of traveling and staying in villages along the way. There seemed to be no sign that the baby was coming, so they continued their journey to Bethlehem. They traveled only a couple hours a day, and would stay in homes of friends or family they knew who lived along the way or they would stay at some of the campsites with other travelers.

"Joseph, how far away are we from Bethlehem?" Miriam asked. She looked up into the sky, and she could tell from where the sun stood that it would probably be dark in the next two to three hours.

"I think we should be there just before the sun sets," Joseph responded. "I see Bethlehem right over there." Joseph pointed into the distance.

"Joseph, I'm not feeling well, do you think we could go a little faster?"

Joseph turned around quickly. "What do you mean?"

She held her breath as she felt another contraction tighten around her stomach. "Miriam, are you okay?" Joseph asked.

Miriam nodded as she winced. "I think so, I mean I don't know ... I'm feeling possible labor pains." She looked up into Joseph's concerned face. "It could be time."

"Time? We should have stayed in Bethany another night!" Joseph groaned and then snapped the reins hard against the donkey's back to get him to quicken his steps. It worked, and the wagon began moving at a faster pace. "At this pace, we should get there much sooner!" Joseph shouted over the noise of the wagon rattling over the dusty rocky road.

Miriam held onto the side of the swaying wagon, feeling more uncomfortable than ever.

Then, without warning, something cracked under the wagon, causing it to topple over onto its side. Miriam and Joseph both fell out. Miriam thankfully had a soft landing on the pillows and was not injured in the process.

Joseph quickly picked himself up and hurried to her side. "Miriam, are you okay?" He took her hand.

"Yes, I'm okay. But what happened?"

They both looked at the broken wheel and axle of the wagon.

"No, how could this happen!" Joseph groaned furiously.

"It's okay. We can just camp here maybe?" Miriam suggested.

"No, we are out of water. We are very close, maybe an hour away. Come and sit on the donkey, and I will lead us there," Joseph said.

He quickly picked up as many items as he could and packed them onto the donkey, laying blankets on its back to make it as comfortable as possible for Miriam. He then lifted her up in his arms and sat her on the donkey.

"There now, soon we will be in Bethlehem." He grabbed the rope that was attached to the harness of the donkey and pulled.

Miriam held tightly to the mane of the donkey as they slowly made their way to Bethlehem.

It seemed like forever until they finally reached the gates of Bethlehem. Joseph continued to lead Miriam and the donkey through the gates and into the bustling little town. The town was crowded with travelers who were there to register for the census and for the holidays. Roman soldiers with their breastplates and helmets with red bristles on top marched around trying to bring order to the crowds. Joseph tried to make his way through the crowd as quickly as possible.

"Joseph son of Jacob! Is that you!" a man about the same age as Joseph shouted over the noise. He pushed through the crowd and nearly pummeled Joseph with a big embrace. "My traitor of a brother!" he teased. "You scoundrel!"

"Matan, son of Dan!" smiled Joseph. "Good to see you too, but I have no time to waste." He gestured to Miriam. "My wife is about to have a baby!"

"She is very beautiful, Joseph!" said Matan. "Well done!" He smiled at Miriam. "But there is no room anywhere in this city! Your mother has opened her home for travelers to stay. Maybe she saved a room for you?" He shrugged.

"Okay, I must take Miriam there right away," Joseph said, tugging the donkey to follow him.

He led her through the streets until they stopped in front of a tall white house.

Miriam moaned as the contractions got tighter and tighter.

Joseph turned to Miriam. "We are here! Welcome to my family's home!" he announced. He led the donkey and Miriam through the gate and into the courtyard where chickens and roosters were clucking defiantly as people were walking in and out of the house.

"It looks like the house is quite full of travelers," said Joseph, stating the obvious. He tied the donkey up to the stable where there was a watering trough for it to drink from. He helped Miriam down onto the ground.

She held onto Joseph's strong arm for balance as she stretched out her cramped legs and body. "Oh, Joseph," she moaned, "it has to be nearly time!" In agony she sat down on a bench by the front door.

Joseph pounded his fist on the heavy wooden door. It swung open.

A small lady with thick grey curls and big brown eyes stood there. She smiled and opened her arms to give Joseph a hug. "Joseph, my son! I was waiting for you to come!" she exclaimed happily. "Though I am sorry, I have taken in so many travelers, but I have saved you a bed in the guest room with some of the other male travelers. Now, come inside. your sister will be happy to see you too!"

"My dear mother!" Joseph quickly gave her a kiss on the cheek. He took her hands in his, then turned her towards Miriam. "Mother, I want you to meet my wife, Miriam. Miriam, this is my mother, Sarah." He turned to his mother. "This is all very sudden, but she is about to give birth right now!"

"Green cucumbers!" Sarah exclaimed and stepped over to Miriam's side. "Nice to meet you, my dear – and soon, my grandchild!" she said with disbelief as she gently felt Miriam's stomach. Miriam recognized the similarities of features that she saw in Joseph.

"My house is brimming with guests," said Sarah, perplexed. "There is not a private room in the house. All my guest rooms are filled with ... several guests!" Then her eyes lit up. "Aha! Come into the stable. I know this is no place to have a baby, but at least you will have your privacy!" She wiped Miriam's damp forehead with her tunic. "Come, Joseph, bring her into the barn. Tamar just cleaned Ezekiel's stable this morning."

Joseph scooped Miriam in his arms and then followed his mother through the stable door. Sarah gathered an armful of hay and laid it down on the earthen floor of the stable stall. Joseph laid Miriam on the hay. Miriam removed her damp headdress and tunic. She looked around the stall and smiled. She didn't care that it was a barn. She was so grateful to have some privacy at last and to be able to move freely.

"Go fetch me a basin of water, quick!" shouted Sarah to Joseph. "And tell Tamar to come help me!"

Joseph quickly did what he was told and ran into the house.

"Thank you ... so much ..." Miriam managed to say between contractions.

"You poor dear, traveling all this way in this condition!" said Sarah, as she helped make Miriam as comfortable as possible. "Tsk! My son better have a good explanation for this!"

Joseph soon returned with his sister at his side. Miriam tried to smile a greeting.

"Tamar, we need some light," said Sarah. "The sun is going down. please fetch some lamps and a clean, sharp knife to cut the cord. The baby is about to deliver any moment now."

She placed her hand on her son's shoulder. "Joseph, if you wouldn't mind leaving this to the women? Why don't you mind the guests for me as I care for your wife?"

Joseph did as she bid.

Meanwhile, Miriam's water broke and she began to push.

As the sun was setting on that cool evening night, in a stable in Bethlehem, the baby, the Messiah was born.

Joseph's mother handed the crying newborn baby to Miriam. "You have a son!" Sarah exclaimed happily. Miriam was glad to see happy tears in Sarah's eyes as she smiled lovingly at Miriam and the baby.

Miriam cuddled the baby in her arms and looked into his sweet little face. His small little cries subsided into little coos. Miriam was filled with wonder and amazement as her heart within her burst with joy and love at the sight of this precious child in her arms. "He's beautiful! The most beautiful sight I have ever seen!" she exclaimed. "My sweet Messiah!" she whispered in his ear as she rocked him lovingly in her arms and then gently kissed him on his head.

"He seems perfectly healthy, such a beautiful babe!" gushed Sarah. "And you also seem healthy as well. I will have Tamar fetch the midwife tomorrow to check on you. Meanwhile, I should go back into the house to care for the guests. I will be back soon!" she kissed Miriam on forehead and then left.

Joseph returned to the stable.

Miriam looked up with a smile. "He's here! The Messiah is here!" she exclaimed happily with tears rolling down her damp cheeks.

Joseph fell to his knees beside Miriam. Miriam carefully placed the baby in his arms.

"I feel so humbled that God would allow me to be a witness of this moment," he said, taking Miriam's hand and giving it a gentle squeeze. "He looks like … just a normal baby, but I feel a presence like I've never felt before. I'm just a Jewish carpenter from Nazareth. Who am I to understand the magnitude of this?"

"I don't know either!" Miriam sniffed back the tears. "All I know is that I feel so much love for this babe and I will do anything to protect him and care for him!"

"You were amazing, my dear," said Joseph. "You are such a strong woman!" He caressed her hair.

Miriam smiled happily.

As Miriam laid down to rest in her bed of hay with the baby in her arms, Joseph took one of the troughs in the barn, cleaned it out and laid some hay and blankets in it. "Here's a bed for the baby." Joseph brought the trough into the stall next to Miriam.

"It's getting a little cold. Is there another blanket by chance?" Miriam asked.

Joseph looked up and saw some swaddling cloth. He dusted it off as much as possible and then handed it to Miriam.

There, they rested with the newborn babe, who lay sleeping in a manger of hay wrapped in swaddling cloth.

Suddenly, there was a knock on the stable door. Miriam had just fed the little babe while Joseph had fallen asleep.

Miriam shook Joseph's shoulder. "Joseph, there's someone at the door of the barn!"

Joseph got up and went to see who it was. He opened the door, and there stood five shepherds with their staffs in hand.

"Sorry to bother you, kind sir, but we heard that there might be a baby that was born in this stable this evening?" a tall skinny shepherd asked.

"Yes, it's true," Joseph said with surprise.

The shepherds looked at each other with excitement.

"Well, you see …" the tall skinny shepherd began enthusiastically, "we were watching our flock this evening in the pasture land outside the city, and —"

"You may say that we are crazy," another shepherd, who was short and hairy piped in, "but suddenly we saw an angel and the glory of God shone around us!" he exclaimed lifting his hands in the air.

"We were very afraid at first, as you can imagine," another scruffy shepherd interjected. "We were just sitting around the fire watching the sheep when suddenly the sky lit up with this angel!"

"The angel said: 'Do not be afraid, for behold, I bring you glad tidings of great joy which will be to all people!'" the skinny tall shepherd spoke up again.

"Listen, he said, that there is born to you this day in the City of David a Savior, who is Christ the Lord," the short fat shepherd interjected again.

Joseph smiled.

" Then the sky was filled with a heavenly host of angels praising God and saying, 'Glory to God in the highest, and on earth peace, good will towards men!'" the tall skinny shepherd lifted his arms in the air.

"You've come to the right place. Come and meet the Messiah of Israel!" Joseph led the way to the stall where Miriam lay next to the manger where the baby lay, wrapped in swaddling cloth.

In the warm glow of the lamps, holy silence filled the stable as they laid their eyes on the precious baby.

"Glory to God in the Highest!" one of the shepherds whispered in awe.

Words can hardly even begin to describe what a moment like this felt like. In the quiet of the stable, away from the commotions within the house full of travelers, resting in an old stable stall on hay was the most glorious sight these shepherds had ever encountered in their lives.

"Peace on earth," the short hairy shepherd followed in tune.

"Goodwill towards men!"

"For unto us this day in the city of David a Messiah is born!"

"Just like the prophets foretold by the prophet Micah: "But you, Bethlehem Ephrathah, though you are small among the clans of Judah, out of you will come for me one who will be the ruler over Israel, whose origins are from of old, from ancient times," he quoted from the prophets.

"Say that again," Miriam spoke up. "Did you say that it was prophesied that the Messiah would be born in Bethlehem?"

"Yes indeed, our Messiah has come, just like the prophets foretold!" He lifted up his hands and looked up heavenward.

Miriam sat back, impressed by the words of the shepherds. This troublesome trip to Bethlehem was actually ordained by God! It was meant to be. The Messiah was meant to be born in Bethlehem. All of this to fulfill the words of the prophet!

"The prophets also said that the Messiah would be born of a virgin," the scruffy shepherd looked at Joseph with a frown.

"That's right. I am a virgin; Joseph has graciously taken me as his wife after I had become miraculously pregnant," Miriam smiled at Joseph lovingly.

"Flying lambs!" one of the shepherds exclaimed. "How is it that we simple shepherds of the sacrificial temple lambs, would be so privileged to meet the Messiah on the day He was born?"

"I feel His Holy presence here. The very crux of the earth's existence has shifted," the tall shepherd said with a choked voice.

"Never knew that I would witness the most historical day of history!" another shepherd piped in.

Each of them took turns putting their hand gently on the baby's forehead to impart a small blessing. They also turned to Joseph and Miriam and blessed them as the new parents and then left.

The next day, Joseph's mother Sarah cleared one of the rooms of the house of all the guests and let Joseph, Miriam, and the baby stay there.

"I'm sorry that you had to give birth in the stable," she apologized to the new parents. "That's not a place for my grandson to be born!" she exclaimed.

Miriam handed the baby to Sarah to hold and cuddle. "When we arrived, I was ready to give birth pretty much anywhere. Thank you for all of your help!" Miriam smiled as she lay down on the new bed.

"You are most welcome, my dear!" beamed Sarah. "Yesterday will be remembered forever!"

"I believe so!" Miriam agreed.

"Well, I am so glad to meet my grandson!" She gave the baby a kiss on the head. "Did those shepherds visit you in the stable last night? They were saying some bizarre things, like angels singing to them in the sky, saying that the Messiah was born, or something like that!" she laughed.

"Yes, indeed they did visit." Miriam looked at Joseph.

"We are living in exciting times, Mother!" Joseph nodded his head.

It was hard for Miriam not to open up and gush out the whole story and proclaim that the baby she was holding was the Messiah of Israel. But at Joseph's bidding, she kept quiet.

Joseph stepped out of the room with his mother. Miriam could hear them speaking quietly to each other.

"So where is Miriam from? Who is her family?" she could hear Sarah say. "You come from the line of David, remember. We just can't just marry anyone!"

"Don't worry, Mother. She also comes from the line of David, not through the line of Solomon, but still through David. And she comes from a very good, God-fearing family. Her father Heli owns an olive oil business in Nazareth and has his own olive press. I think you should be very proud of my choice."

"I'm happy to hear this." Then she added sweetly, "She is also very beautiful and seems to be very kind."

"She really is, and most of all we love each other very much." Joseph responded. Miriam blushed happily. Her new mama's heart felt like it was going to burst.

As was the Jewish custom, on the eighth day after the baby was born, Joseph invited the local Rabbi to the house for the baby's circumcision. A few people showed up for the circumcision. And some of the guests who were staying at the house also attended the ceremony.

After the deed was done, the Rabbi blessed the baby and handed him to Miriam and Joseph.

"And what will the baby's name be?" the Rabbi asked.

"His name will be Yeshua (Jesus)." Joseph announced.

"What a name!" Joseph's mother declared.

Afterwards they had a small feast for everyone. Miriam met many of Joseph's old friends. Many people spoke highly of him to her. But when Miriam listened in on Joseph's conversations, she could hear them scolding him for leaving Bethlehem and trying to convince him to return permanently. Joseph argued with them, but they were very stubborn in their opinions.

As time went on, they continued to live with Joseph's mother Sarah in Bethlehem. She was very helpful with the baby, which allowed Miriam plenty of rest. And in return, Joseph was a huge help in making repairs around the house and helping his mother with different affairs that related to her home and helping her with her hospitality business. It was interesting for Miriam to see Joseph in his town of birth. He was well respected in the town, and everyone was interested in his opinions, especially in politics. Miriam could tell he was getting tired of talking about politics and listening to people's opinions.

When Miriam's days of purification were complete, Joseph and Miriam traveled to Jerusalem to the Holy Temple where they would present the baby to the Lord. It was customary according to the law of Moses that every firstborn male be consecrated to the Lord, by sacrificing a pair of turtle doves or pigeons.

Miriam held Joseph's arm with one arm, and with the other arm she held the baby Yeshua. As they climbed the stairs to the Temple, Miriam remembered her last visit to the Temple with Zachariah. So much had happened since that time and here she was again, but this time with her beloved husband by her side and the precious Messiah in her arms!

When they walked through the gate Beautiful, an elderly man with a long white beard approached Miriam and Joseph. "Dearly beloved!" he said kindly. "I'm sorry to bother you, but my name is Simeon. May I?" He held out his arms to hold the baby Yeshua.

Miriam looked at Joseph not knowing what to do since she did not know the man. Joseph nodded his head, so Miriam carefully placed Yeshua in the elderly man's arms.

Simeon looked lovingly at the baby. To Miriam's surprise she saw a tear stream down his weathered cheek. He then lifted up the baby to heaven and prayed out loud: "Bless the Lord, now you are letting Your servant depart in peace, according to Your Word! For my eyes have seen Your salvation! This which You have prepared before the face of all peoples, a light to bring revelation to the Gentiles, and the glory of Your people Israel!"

Joseph and Miriam marveled at the man's words.

"Thank you, Rabbi!" Joseph said.

The man gently kissed the baby on the head and then handed the baby back to Miriam. Then looked directly into Miriam's eyes. "Behold, this Child is destined for the fall and rising of many in Israel, and for a sign which will be spoken against, and yes, a sword shall pierce through your own soul also, and the thoughts of many hearts shall be revealed."

Miriam didn't know what to say in response or what he meant by his words, but she knew they held great truth and weight.

"These are profound words," Joseph said as he shook the man's hand.

"I was told from above that I would see the Messiah before I pass," smiled Simeon, wiping the tears from his eyes. "Salvation is here!"

Miriam and Joseph thanked him and continued to make their way to one of the priests for the consecration.

Miriam leaned over to Joseph. "First Elizabeth and Zachariah. Then the shepherds, and now this!" she exclaimed.

"It's unexplainable!" said Joseph, shaking his head in amazement.

After they had completed the sacrifice of the turtle doves and consecrated Yeshua before one of the priests, they began their departure. As they reached the Beautiful Gate to leave, Miriam recognized an older lady who stood by the gate. As long as Miriam could remember, she had seen this lady at the Temple at each visit. She was always there, worshipping, fasting and praying. Miriam had heard stories about her, that she was named Anna, the daughter of Penuel of the tribe of Asher. And that after seven years of marriage she had become widowed. Miriam had never talked to her, but knew of her and had seen her many times.

Suddenly Anna noticed the young couple and baby and began to make her way towards them. Miriam knew right away that she also knew. With Joseph holding the baby, Miriam met Anna with an embrace.

"Praise be to God who has brought salvation for His people and redemption for Jerusalem!" Anna cried out in a loud voice for everyone around her to hear. "Blessed is He who comes in the Name of the Lord!"

Miriam felt overwhelmed and began to cry. On one hand she felt extremely privileged to be the mother of the Messiah, but on the other hand she felt completely incapable of such a task! She had no power to make things happen in her own strength and had no idea of things to come or what the Son of God would do. Each of these confirmations strengthened her faith but also filled her with holy fear to do everything righteously. She was so grateful for Joseph who helped keep her on the right track, and would often remind her to care for the

Messiah's basic needs and allow God to do what He intended to do. It wasn't up to her to make sure Yeshua fulfils His destiny.

That night as Miriam rocked her baby to sleep, she pondered over the encounter with the shepherds, of Simeon and Anna at the Temple. She looked at the baby Yeshua.

"You know you are no ordinary baby," she whispered. "All I know is that you will somehow bring salvation to us. I have no idea how or when. So please forgive your little mama for her ignorance in times to come. I have no idea what I am doing." Miriam laughed to herself. "We have longed for you since the beginning of time and I am so glad you are here now!"

Suddenly there was a knock on the door. Joseph went to answer it. Then he turned back to Miriam, who could see that there was someone hiding behind Joseph.

"We have a guest!" Joseph announced with a smile.

Heli, Miriam's father, stepped out from behind Joseph. His eyes were wide with awe.

"Abba! What are you doing here? It is the olive harvest time!" Miriam said in surprise.

"Who knows how many days we have on earth, dear daughter! I just had to come and see this promised seed of Jesse!"

Miriam carefully laid the sleeping baby in his arms. Then she hugged her father.

"This is just the beginning, my dear children, just the beginning," Heli repeated.

As time went on, Miriam and Joseph continued to care for baby Yeshua throughout his childhood and young adulthood.

They ended up staying in Bethlehem with Joseph's mother longer than planned.

While they were still there, some unexpected guests came looking for them. They were Magi from the East, who showed up bearing expensive gifts of gold, frankincense and myrrh. They told them they had followed a star from the East. Not knowing where to go, they had sought guidance from King Herod, asking him where they could find the "King of the Jews". As a result of their inquiry, King Herod grew paranoid and ordered that all male babies under the age of two in Bethlehem be executed.

Before the execution played out, an angel warned Joseph in a dream and told them to go to Egypt to escape King Herod's evil plan. They did as the angel bid them to do, and escaped to Egypt and lived there for a couple of months. Joseph received yet another dream saying that those who tried to kill the baby had now passed away. Thus they then returned back to their home in Nazareth where Joseph reopened his carpentry business, and they settled back into their little home.

After the adjustment of moving back to Nazareth, Miriam was sitting in the shade of an olive tree outside their house. She was busy sewing a new garment for their growing little boy, while little Yeshua was busy playing with some wooden animals that Joseph had hand carved for him.

Suddenly a wagon with two horses pulled up to the house. Miriam laid down her sewing and picked Yeshua up in her arms. She curiously looked to see who were the unexpected guests. The driver of the wagon hopped down and opened up the back of the wagon and placed a foot stool down on the ground. Then a refine young woman stepped out of the wagon. Mary recognised her immediately!

" Rachel!" Miriam gasped in surprise. She rushed over to the wagon to greet her. They embraced and gave one another a kiss on each cheek.

" My dear! It is good to finally see you! And you!" Rachel tickled Yeshua's little belly which caused him to erupt into giggles.

"I am so honoured that you would visit me! Please come in for tea!" Miriam welcomed her into her home.

" I can't stay for long, but I really wanted to see you again and meet this little guy!!" Rachel followed her into her home. " I've been trying to trace you down for quite some time now."

" You were looking for me?" Miriam asked surprised.

" Yes of course. I mean… you left such an impression on me, and I've thought about you many times." Rachel said. Miriam blushed. She was amazed that someone with such nobility and affluence would even consider her; a humble young woman from a humble little town.

" You are too kind! But really, I am the one indebted here. You provided a safe passage for me during a very precarious time in my life. And I have treasured the beautiful blue scarf that you gave me!" Miriam said while she was preparing some tea and some light refreshments.

" Please, it was nothing!" Rachel waved her hand. She then bent down next to Yeshua and looked at him intently.

" Tell me Miriam, is this the Messiah?" she asked. Miriam stopped in her tracks and looked over at the two of them. So much had transpired since her last encounter with Rachel at the Holy Temple in Jerusalem. She agreed that by just looking at Yeshua, one might not recognise who He truly was, but in her heart she knew He was indeed special and had a unique destiny that awaited him.

" Yes He is. " Miriam said with surety in her voice. She then sat down with Rachel and told the whole story from beginning to present day.

" Wow, what an extraordinary story, almost unreal! It is a story that will never be forgotten through the ages! So interesting about the shepherds and the Magi showing up mysteriously." Rachel shook her head in amazement. "I've never heard anything like it before in my life! It gives me a sense of wonder and hope that God has not forgotten us." She mused thoughtfully. Then she looked up at Rachel intently. " So now what?"

Miriam paused to think. Being back in her home of Nazareth, life almost seemed ordinary again. Being a wife and mother seemed to be her main concern at the moment, but she knew that even if things seemed more normal now, she was still serving a higher purpose in caring for little Yeshua.

" We are trusting in God. He will bring about His destiny." she responded thoughtfully.

" I am very curious to see how things unfold!" Rachel caressed Yeshua's head of dark curls. " To just think… you may be kissing the face of God!"

A hushed silence filled the room, as they both thought about what the future might hold for them and for the world around them. How will this precious sweet little boy bring peace and restoration to their people and the whole world? Only time will tell…

One thing for sure… the Messiah had come!

SCRIPTURE REFERENCES

Isaiah 7:13
Then he said, "Hear now, O house of David! *Is it* a small thing for you to weary men, but will you weary my God also? Therefore the Lord Himself will give you a sign: Behold, the virgin shall conceive and bear a Son, and shall call His name Immanuel.

Isaiah 9:6-7
For unto us a Child is born,
Unto us a Son is given;
And the government will be upon His shoulder.
And His name will be called
Wonderful, Counselor, Mighty God,
Everlasting Father, Prince of Peace.

Of the increase of *His* government and peace
There will be no end,
Upon the throne of David and over His kingdom,
To order it and establish it with judgment and justice
From that time forward, even forever.
The zeal of the Lord of hosts will perform this.

Micah 5:2
"But you, Bethlehem Ephrathah,
Though you are little among the thousands of Judah,
Yet out of you shall come forth to Me
The One to be Ruler in Israel,
Whose goings forth *are* from of old,
From everlasting."

Matthew 1
The book of the genealogy of Jesus Christ, the Son of David, the Son of Abraham:
2 Abraham begot Isaac, Isaac begot Jacob, and Jacob begot Judah and his brothers. **3** Judah begot Perez and Zerah by Tamar, Perez begot Hezron, and Hezron begot

Ram. **4** Ram begot Amminadab, Amminadab begot Nahshon, and Nahshon begot Salmon. **5** Salmon begot Boaz by Rahab, Boaz begot Obed by Ruth, Obed begot Jesse, **6** and Jesse begot David the king.

David the king begot Solomon by her *who had been the wife* of Uriah. **7** Solomon begot Rehoboam, Rehoboam begot Abijah, and Abijah begot Asa. **8** Asa begot Jehoshaphat, Jehoshaphat begot Joram, and Joram begot Uzziah. **9** Uzziah begot Jotham, Jotham begot Ahaz, and Ahaz begot Hezekiah. **10** Hezekiah begot Manasseh, Manasseh begot Amon, and Amon begot Josiah. **11** Josiah begot Jeconiah and his brothers about the time they were carried away to Babylon.

12 And after they were brought to Babylon, Jeconiah begot Shealtiel, and Shealtiel begot Zerubbabel. **13** Zerubbabel begot Abiud, Abiud begot Eliakim, and Eliakim begot Azor. **14** Azor begot Zadok, Zadok begot Achim, and Achim begot Eliud. **15** Eliud begot Eleazar, Eleazar begot Matthan, and Matthan begot Jacob. **16** And Jacob begot Joseph the husband of Miriam, of whom was born Jesus who is called Christ.

17 So all the generations from Abraham to David *are* fourteen generations, from David until the captivity in Babylon *are* fourteen generations, and from the captivity in Babylon until the Christ *are* fourteen generations.

Christ Born of Miriam **18** Now the birth of Jesus Christ was as follows: After His mother Miriam was betrothed to Joseph, before they came together, she was found with child of the Holy Spirit. **19** Then Joseph her husband, being a just *man,* and not wanting to make her a public example, was minded to put her away secretly. **20** But while he thought about these things, behold, an angel of the Lord appeared to him in a dream, saying, "Joseph, son of David, do not be afraid to take to you Miriam your wife, for that which is conceived in her is of the Holy Spirit. **21** And she will bring forth a Son, and you shall call His name Jesus, for He will save His people from their sins."

22 So all this was done that it might be fulfilled which was spoken by the Lord through the prophet, saying: **23** "Behold, the virgin shall be with child, and bear a Son, and they shall call His name Immanuel," which is translated, "God with us."
24 Then Joseph, being aroused from sleep, did as the angel of the Lord commanded him and took to him his wife, **25** and did not know her till she had brought forth her firstborn Son. And he called His name Jesus.

Matthew 2

Now after Jesus was born in Bethlehem of Judea in the days of Herod the king, behold, wise men from the East came to Jerusalem, **2** saying, "Where is He who has been born King of the Jews? For we have seen His star in the East and have come to worship Him."
3 When Herod the king heard *this,* he was troubled, and all Jerusalem with him. **4** And when he had gathered all the chief priests and scribes of the people together, he inquired of them where the Christ was to be born.
5 So they said to him, "In Bethlehem of Judea, for thus it is written by the prophet:
6 'But you, Bethlehem, *in* the land of Judah,
Are not the least among the rulers of Judah;
For out of you shall come a Ruler
Who will shepherd My people Israel.' "
7 Then Herod, when he had secretly called the wise men, determined from them what time the star appeared. **8** And he sent them to Bethlehem and said, "Go and search carefully for the young Child, and when you have found *Him,* bring back word to me, that I may come and worship Him also."
9 When they heard the king, they departed; and behold, the star which they had seen in the East went before them, till it came and stood over where the young Child was. **10** When they saw the star, they rejoiced with exceedingly great joy. **11** And when they had come into the house, they saw the young Child with Miriam His

mother, and fell down and worshiped Him. And when they had opened their treasures, they presented gifts to Him: gold, frankincense, and myrrh.

12 Then, being divinely warned in a dream that they should not return to Herod, they departed for their own country another way.

The Flight into Egypt

13 Now when they had departed, behold, an angel of the Lord appeared to Joseph in a dream, saying, "Arise, take the young Child and His mother, flee to Egypt, and stay there until I bring you word; for Herod will seek the young Child to destroy Him."

14 When he arose, he took the young Child and His mother by night and departed for Egypt, **15** and was there until the death of Herod, that it might be fulfilled which was spoken by the Lord through the prophet, saying, "Out of Egypt I called My Son."

Massacre of the Innocents

16 Then Herod, when he saw that he was deceived by the wise men, was exceedingly angry; and he sent forth and put to death all the male children who were in Bethlehem and in all its districts, from two years old and under, according to the time which he had determined from the wise men. **17** Then was fulfilled what was spoken by Jeremiah the prophet, saying:

18 "A voice was heard in Ramah,

Lamentation, weeping, and great mourning,

Rachel weeping *for* her children,

Refusing to be comforted,

Because they are no more."

The Home in Nazareth

19 Now when Herod was dead, behold, an angel of the Lord appeared in a dream to Joseph in Egypt, **20** saying, "Arise, take the young Child and His mother, and go to the land of Israel, for those who sought the young Child's life are dead." **21** Then he arose, took the young Child and His mother, and came into the land of Israel.

22 But when he heard that Archelaus was reigning over Judea instead of his father Herod, he was afraid to go there. And being warned by God in a dream, he turned aside into the region of Galilee. **23** And he came and dwelt in a city called Nazareth, that it might be fulfilled which was spoken by the prophets, "He shall be called a Nazarene."

Luke 1: 5 - 80:

5 There was in the days of Herod, the king of Judea, a certain priest named Zacharias, of the division of Abijah. His wife *was* of the daughters of Aaron, and her name *was* Elizabeth. **6** And they were both righteous before God, walking in all the commandments and ordinances of the Lord blameless. **7** But they had no child, because Elizabeth was barren, and they were both well advanced in years.

8 So it was, that while he was serving as priest before God in the order of his division, **9** according to the custom of the priesthood, his lot fell to burn incense when he went into the temple of the Lord. **10** And the whole multitude of the people was praying outside at the hour of incense. **11** Then an angel of the Lord appeared to him, standing on the right side of the altar of incense. **12** And when Zacharias saw *him,* he was troubled, and fear fell upon him.

13 But the angel said to him, "Do not be afraid, Zacharias, for your prayer is heard; and your wife Elizabeth will bear you a son, and you shall call his name John. **14** And you will have joy and gladness, and many will rejoice at his birth. **15** For he will be great in the sight of the Lord, and shall drink neither wine nor strong drink. He will also be filled with the Holy Spirit, even from his mother's womb. **16** And he will turn many of the children of Israel to the Lord their God. **17** He will also go before Him in the spirit and power of Elijah, 'to turn the hearts of the fathers to the children,' and the disobedient to the wisdom of the just, to make ready a people prepared for the Lord."

18 And Zacharias said to the angel, "How shall I know this? For I am an old man, and my wife is well advanced in years."

19 And the angel answered and said to him, "I am Gabriel, who stands in the presence of God, and was sent to speak to you and bring you these glad tidings. **20** But behold, you will be mute and not able to speak until the day these things take place, because you did not believe my words which will be fulfilled in their own time."

21 And the people waited for Zacharias, and marvelled that he lingered so long in the temple. **22** But when he came out, he could not speak to them; and they perceived that he had seen a vision in the temple, for he beckoned to them and remained speechless.

23 So it was, as soon as the days of his service were completed, that he departed to his own house. **24** Now after those days his wife Elizabeth conceived; and she hid herself five months, saying, **25** "Thus the Lord has dealt with me, in the days when He looked on *me,* to take away my reproach among people."

26 Now in the sixth month the angel Gabriel was sent by God to a city of Galilee named Nazareth, **27** to a virgin betrothed to a man whose name was Joseph, of the house of David. The virgin's name *was* Miriam. **28** And having come in, the angel said to her, "Rejoice, highly favored *one,* the Lord *is* with you; blessed *are* you among women!"

29 But when she saw *him,* she was troubled at his saying, and considered what manner of greeting this was. **30** Then the angel said to her, "Do not be afraid, Miriam, for you have found favor with God. **31** And behold, you will conceive in your womb and bring forth a Son, and shall call His name Jesus. **32** He will be great, and will be called the Son of the Highest; and the Lord God will give Him the throne of His father David.

33 And He will reign over the house of Jacob forever, and of His kingdom there will be no end."
34 Then Miriam said to the angel, "How can this be, since I do not know a man?"
35 And the angel answered and said to her, "*The* Holy Spirit will come upon you, and the power of the Highest will overshadow you; therefore, also, that Holy One who is to be born will be called the Son of God. **36** Now indeed, Elizabeth your relative has also conceived a son in her old age; and this is now the sixth month for her who was called barren. **37** For with God nothing will be impossible."
38 Then Miriam said, "Behold the maidservant of the Lord! Let it be to me according to your word." And the angel departed from her.

Miriam Visits Elizabeth

39 Now Miriam arose in those days and went into the hill country with haste, to a city of Judah, **40** and entered the house of Zacharias and greeted Elizabeth. **41** And it happened, when Elizabeth heard the greeting of Miriam, that the babe leaped in her womb; and Elizabeth was filled with the Holy Spirit. **42** Then she spoke out with a loud voice and said, "Blessed *are* you among women, and blessed *is* the fruit of your womb! **43** But why *is* this *granted* to me, that the mother of my Lord should come to me? **44** For indeed, as soon as the voice of your greeting sounded in my ears, the babe leaped in my womb for joy. **45** Blessed *is* she who believed, for there will be a fulfillment of those things which were told her from the Lord."

The Song of Miriam

46 And Miriam said:
"My soul magnifies the Lord,
47 And my spirit has rejoiced in God my Savior.
48 For He has regarded the lowly state of His maidservant;
For behold, henceforth all generations will call me blessed.

49 For He who is mighty has done great things for me,
And holy *is* His name.
50 And His mercy *is* on those who fear Him
From generation to generation.
51 He has shown strength with His arm;
He has scattered *the* proud in the imagination of their hearts.
52 He has put down the mighty from *their* thrones,
And exalted *the* lowly.
53 He has filled *the* hungry with good things,
And *the* rich He has sent away empty.
54 He has helped His servant Israel,
In remembrance of *His* mercy,
55 As He spoke to our fathers,
To Abraham and to his seed forever."
56 And Miriam remained with her about three months, and returned to her house.

Birth of John the Baptist

57 Now Elizabeth's full time came for her to be delivered, and she brought forth a son. **58** When her neighbors and relatives heard how the Lord had shown great mercy to her, they rejoiced with her.
59 So it was, on the eighth day, that they came to circumcise the child; and they would have called him by the name of his father, Zacharias. **60** His mother answered and said, "No; he shall be called John."
61 But they said to her, "There is no one among your relatives who is called by this name." **62** So they made signs to his father—what he would have him called.
63 And he asked for a writing tablet, and wrote, saying, "His name is John." So they all marveled. **64** Immediately his mouth was opened and his tongue *loosed,* and he spoke, praising God. **65** Then fear came on all who dwelt around them; and all these sayings were discussed throughout all the hill country of Judea. **66** And all those who heard *them* kept *them* in their hearts, saying, "What kind of child will this be?" And the hand of the Lord was with him.

67 Now his father Zacharias was filled with the Holy Spirit, and prophesied, saying:
68 "Blessed *is* the Lord God of Israel,
For He has visited and redeemed His people,
69 And has raised up a horn of salvation for us
In the house of His servant David,
70 As He spoke by the mouth of His holy prophets,
Who *have been* since the world began,
71 That we should be saved from our enemies
And from the hand of all who hate us,
72 To perform the mercy *promised* to our fathers
And to remember His holy covenant,
73 The oath which He swore to our father Abraham:
74 To grant us that we,
Being delivered from the hand of our enemies,
Might serve Him without fear,
75 In holiness and righteousness before Him all the days of our life.
76 "And you, child, will be called the prophet of the Highest;
For you will go before the face of the Lord to prepare His ways,
77 To give knowledge of salvation to His people
By the remission of their sins,
78 Through the tender mercy of our God,
With which the Dayspring from on high has visited us;
79 To give light to those who sit in darkness and the shadow of death,
To guide our feet into the way of peace."
80 So the child grew and became strong in spirit, and was in the deserts till the day of his manifestation to Israel.

Luke 2: 1 - 40:
And it came to pass in those days *that* a decree went out from Caesar Augustus that all the world should be registered. **2** This census first took place while Quirinius

was governing Syria. **3** So all went to be registered, everyone to his own city.

4 Joseph also went up from Galilee, out of the city of Nazareth, into Judea, to the city of David, which is called Bethlehem, because he was of the house and lineage of David, **5** to be registered with Miriam, his betrothed wife, who was with child. **6** So it was, that while they were there, the days were completed for her to be delivered. **7** And she brought forth her firstborn Son, and wrapped Him in swaddling cloths, and laid Him in a manger, because there was no room for them in the inn.

8 Now there were in the same country shepherds living out in the fields, keeping watch over their flock by night. **9** And behold, an angel of the Lord stood before them, and the glory of the Lord shone around them, and they were greatly afraid. **10** Then the angel said to them, "Do not be afraid, for behold, I bring you good tidings of great joy which will be to all people. **11** For there is born to you this day in the city of David a Savior, who is Christ the Lord. **12** And this *will be* the sign to you: You will find a Babe wrapped in swaddling cloths, lying in a manger."

13 And suddenly there was with the angel a multitude of the heavenly host praising God and saying:

14

"Glory to God in the highest,
And on earth peace, goodwill toward men!"

15 So it was, when the angels had gone away from them into heaven, that the shepherds said to one another, "Let us now go to Bethlehem and see this thing that has come to pass, which the Lord has made known to us." **16** And they came with haste and found Miriam and Joseph, and the Babe lying in a manger. **17** Now when they had seen *Him,* they made widely known the saying which was told them concerning this Child. **18** And all those who heard *it* marveled at those things which were told them by the shepherds. **19** But Miriam kept all these things and pondered *them* in her heart. **20** Then the shepherds returned, glorifying and praising God for all the things that they had heard and seen, as it was told them.

21 And when eight days were completed for the circumcision of the Child, His name was called Jesus, the name given by the angel before He was conceived in the womb.

22 Now when the days of her purification according to the law of Moses were completed, they brought Him to Jerusalem to present *Him* to the Lord **23** (as it is written in the law of the Lord, "Every male who opens the womb shall be called holy to the Lord"), **24** and to offer a sacrifice according to what is said in the law of the Lord, "A pair of turtledoves or two young pigeons."

25 And behold, there was a man in Jerusalem whose name *was* Simeon, and this man *was* just and devout, waiting for the Consolation of Israel, and the Holy Spirit was upon him. **26** And it had been revealed to him by the Holy Spirit that he would not see death before he had seen the Lord's Christ. **27** So he came by the Spirit into the temple. And when the parents brought in the Child Jesus, to do for Him according to the custom of the law, **28** he took Him up in his arms and blessed God and said:
29

"Lord, now You are letting Your servant depart in peace, According to Your word;
30

For my eyes have seen Your salvation
31

Which You have prepared before the face of all peoples,
32

A light to *bring* revelation to the Gentiles,
And the glory of Your people Israel."

33 And Joseph and His mother marveled at those things which were spoken of Him. **34** Then Simeon blessed them, and said to Miriam His mother, "Behold, this *Child* is destined for the fall and rising of many in Israel, and for a sign which will be spoken against **35** (yes, a

sword will pierce through your own soul also), that the thoughts of many hearts may be revealed."
36 Now there was one, Anna, a prophetess, the daughter of Phanuel, of the tribe of Asher. She was of a great age, and had lived with a husband seven years from her virginity; **37** and this woman *was* a widow of about eighty-four years, who did not depart from the temple, but served *God* with fastings and prayers night and day. **38** And coming in that instant she gave thanks to [j]the Lord, and spoke of Him to all those who looked for redemption in Jerusalem.
39 So when they had performed all things according to the law of the Lord, they returned to Galilee, to their *own* city, Nazareth. **40** And the Child grew and became strong in spirit, filled with wisdom; and the grace of God was upon Him.

ABOUT THE AUTHOR

Deanna Malespin was born in Canada and later studied at a university in Israel. During her studies, she married the love of her life and ended up settling in the Galilee with her husband Chaim and her three children Matiah, Hadar and Nadav (who was born close to the release of this book!).

Manufactured by Amazon.ca
Bolton, ON